THE///
///ENDLESS
DRIFT///

:::

Towns

Endless thanks to my Mom, Katie, and all my friends and family who have made this and everything else in my life possible.

THE///
///ENDLESS
DRIFT///

PART ONE

COLLIDE

Now and again, I see the same thing. Sitting inside my mind I stare disconnected at a life playing out in front of me as it melts away in endless drips that make no impact upon what it is that I believe to be myself, which I believe to be nothing at all.

Every morning I wake up to the sound of existence humming ceaseless notes into my ear. I rise to the day, which will inevitably bring upon me a pointlessness so numbing I lose all contempt for it. I fall, listlessly, through this distant life. I've become detached to everything but my vague thoughts, which push and pull me around until I wake in the middle of being. When thrown into this life, I feel surrounded by an all too familiar existence, an existence that is completely separate from me yet at the same time everything that I am.

People talk to me and I hear nothing. Instead of paying attention to what is said, I'm staring at the light as it falls in empty colors on the objects around me. I'm listening to the way the walls echo sounds into my head. I'm lost in thoughts about nothing at all.

People take me as quiet, calm, and reserved.

All that I actually am is empty.

Emotions do live and die within me, however, and in wild movements they thrash about my mind. Mostly I watch them as they die in vain and litter the depths of my consciousness, turning into suffocating heaps of apathy. Sometimes, though, they grace a small part of me that's still connected. For a moment I feel pain. I feel joy. I feel a thriving building up within me and I feel joined with this life. Nevertheless, the feeling fades, much like everything else, and again I drift apart.

I often wonder if something is wrong with me. Am I supposed to feel more attached to life? Everyone around me seems to be. They live in a different way than I do. They thrive upon the endless fleeting moments that scatter their lives. The thoughts within my head feel distant to the world in which they live.

But maybe I'm just a cynical twenty something, masking my emotions with indifference just to feel a little more unique, more alone.

Since I was young, I've been different from most of the people around me. I've lived in books about life and death, meaning and reality. Throughout my teenage years I thought I was a Buddhist. In college I was a devout philosopher. After leaving school I was an artist living within life's beauty.

Now I am nothing.

Now I am no one.

My life is not entirely a dull mess. Moments of pleasure do occur, and right now happens to be one of them. The sun is falling as it throws a dying, golden light over everything within its reach. I'm sitting on the curb in front of my apartment, smoking a cigarette and watching as the smoke fades away into nothing. Children are playing down the street, yelling at each other in a language I don't recognize, but the happiness in their voices I can understand. It's something I've lost and something I have to find again.

Or maybe I don't?

Maybe it's something I have to learn to lose.

A cool breeze blows across my face.

It's September, the twenty-fifth one for me, and the air outside is crisp. I look upwards and watch the changing sky as I exhale the last of my cigarette. A few clouds pass by with hints of colors that have no name.

I stop my thoughts and stare.

Vaguely, I feel time pulling me towards something I can't understand, or maybe I do. I feel the impression of an unknown past and at the same time the forming of a familiar future.

Sensations collide as the present turns into eternity.

The feeling I get is so subtle that it dances just barely on the edge of my consciousness, yet so captivating it engulfs and becomes everything that I am.

I've been here before.

I'll be here again.

I'm caught in this sensation, for how long I don't know, until it slips away inside of me. The memory of it feels so foreign it's as if it never happened. I sit confused with the feeling I've just returned from far away, deep inside myself.

The phone in my pocket rings and for a moment I ignore it. I'm stuck in thought about what has happened. It soon fades and I'm stranded in my empty mind, looking out at nothing.

What is this?

SPINNING

My friends seem more like distant neighbors with whom the only connections shared are complaints about the present and memories of the past. Getting fucked up is the only way to feel comfortable around each other anymore. A bottle and a joint melt us together into a sad attempt at socializing.

A weekend has come and I'm at a house I've known for far too long. Laughter fills the rooms. I join in with a smile that hides my drifting mind. A cynicism is building up inside me, but I don't let it take hold. It yells at me from afar, about the people I see and the things they say. I stare blankly at the wall until it gives up and dies. Conversations pile upon themselves, while the words being spoken make a chorus of sounds that drench any thoughts that happen in my mind.

I drink.

I talk to people and people talk to me. A girl tells me about the traffic she faces everyday and the construction that makes her life so difficult. Someone else talks to me about the way the air smells outside before they go to work. My friend, whom owns the house I'm in, asks where Ashley is and I tell him that she's out of town, which she is. She's visiting her family in a place no one's ever heard of.

What's mostly said is pointless to me, and I feel slightly shitty for thinking of it that way. I start to question everything about myself and stare into a dusty lamp sitting on a corner table. Its light is caught beneath a dirty shell of cheap stained glass. I feel strange, either from the awkward connection between me and the lamp or from the beer I've been drinking. I get up to go outside before I turn into a dazed lump of something in front of everyone.

A friend and I are sitting together on the patio. Pale yellow shines outward from the lights behind us. Music and voices mix inside the house to make a muffled sound of something pour out through the walls. A half empty green bottle sits in my hand.

I stare at my feet.

"I can't do it anymore," he says, "Everyday I just sit and listen to them talk about some shit I already know." He takes a drink. "I'd rather just work some job I don't care about and spend my free time throwing my life down the drain. At least I'd get some enjoyment out of all this."

"Are you gonna quit?" I ask.

"Yea man. I am," he replies.

I nod and stare out into the yard. His chair makes small, broken noises as he shifts his weight around. I remember when I left school. The night I spent lying awake, alone. I dreamt without sleep of what my life would be.

Light from the world behind us catches my bottle and I take a drink.

"So how's life?" he asks me.

"Its alright," I reply, "Pretty much just working most of the time. You've got that to look forward to once you quit. If you stay in school you at least have an excuse for not having a job."

"That's true," he says.

We sit in silence and I try to think of something to say. I give up and finish my beer.

"So what's your plan?" he asks.

"I mean, you know. The whole art thing," I reply, "and the music. I'm working on it."

"Your shit's good man. I mean it," he tells me, "I was listening to your music the other day. It would be better if it had words though. Ya know? I mean people have to connect with it more."

"Yea," I say.

"Nothing wrong with selling your stuff," he tells me.

I nod again and pretend to think. I hate talking about myself. I get a feeling that the more people tell me how to do something, the less it becomes mine. When the subject is my life, I ignore what's being said as a reflex. It's a flinching within my mind to hide myself from being polluted, as if there was a pureness inside me to begin with.

I take a drink from my empty bottle.

"I'm getting another," I tell him as I stand up to go inside. I trip a little on the bottom of my chair.

I feel my thoughts spinning out of my mouth as I talk about things I don't understand.

I drink. I laugh. I drink.

There's music and I'm dancing. Or something. Maybe I'm falling and catching myself over and over again. Either way it works and I'm feeling fine. People are all around me. I'm doing nothing. I'm doing something.

No one is around me.

I'm sitting drunk and alone in front of the house. Rolling around in my mind and laughing to myself, I pull out a cigarette and somehow get it lit.

"What!" I yell to myself and everything else. I begin to laugh and take a long drag from my cigarette. The yard that I was staring at spins out of sight. Now the concrete below me, with its slightly blue tint from the moonlight, is all that I see. The door behind me opens and a girl I've known since I was young walks by.

"Since when do you smoke?" she asks.

"Since I started smoking," I reply.

"That's not you."

"Yea, I guess, but oh well."

"Well you should stop. Why aren't you inside?"

"It's nice out"

"Whatever," she says as she walks away. I watch her. Maybe I don't know her, but she knows me. I see concrete again and finish the last of my cigarette.

"It is fucking nice out," I say.

She's gone though, and it reaches no one. I light another cigarette.

I'm drunk. I'm really drunk. I'm really fucking drunk. I need another drink because I need to be even more really fucking drunk so I can feel like I'm an artist or something and I have no reason or meaning in my life and that's the reason and meaning of my life. I'm taking a piss on the side of the house and drawing mountains from China on the brick with my piss. I get a little on my foot and rub it off in the wet grass. I look at the mountains but they've since run down and look more like bleeding St. Louis arches and it depresses me and I laugh because it makes me feel like a depressed artist.

"I'm a fucking hypocrite or something," I say to no one.

"Why man?"

I'm confused.

I walk around the corner and see my friend lying in the grass.

"Why are you a hypocrite or something man?"

"Because I think I feel nothing and that's what's really happening. I do feel things. I'm just intellectually detached. I know. I know. I only know that I'm not this. Not by experience. You're gonna get wet or something and bugs will crawl on you by the way."

"Probably," he says while lying still.

"But I mean, not by experience, but by thoughts and thinking," I tell him as I lean on whatever it is that's next to me, "It's like I feel things too much. So dumb. That sounded so dumb."

"Probably."

"I mean, it's like I only think I don't feel things when I really do feel them. That's why I'm so depressed all the damn time and I just think I'm really empty but I'm really depressed all the time. I'm not enlightened or anything. I don't really feel detached. I just think I am. And it makes me think I feel I am."

"You're talking a lot," he says as he turns his head to the other side.

"Yeah. But maybe I really don't feel anything. Maybe I think not feeling anything should feel better. It's stupid. Everyday is stupid. The same thing all the time is stupid."

I remember I should be drunk and fall down on top of him. Two grown men lying on top of each other in the front lawn.

I laugh.

I'm standing back inside the house and people are drunk but I know they're not as drunk as me. I'm really fucking drunk. I lean on the wall and hold my beer and try to look cool. I give up and sit down next to someone. They ask me something and I tell them something. I can't remember what they said or what I said, while it was being said.

I can't stand it.

The pointlessness.

Constantly pushing me forward into more and more pointlessness.

Why?

There's no fucking reason why.

I listen to the sound of people talking as I fade out into nothing.

I'm at home, lying on the floor beside my bed. With my eyes closed I watch as the darkness spins. I open my left eye and see the carpet laying out before me like a plain of white grass shining in blue moonlight. I laugh to myself and disappear.

FERRIS

I'm falling, but I'm also standing still. The floor is falling actually, and I'm standing on it. I know this because the walls are moving upwards. But I suppose that doesn't mean I'm falling. It's actually that the walls are flying. I must be wrong. The walls aren't flying. That's impossible. The floor must be falling. There's a naked woman and I think I know who she is but I also think I don't. She's close, asking me something and touching me. I'm close, telling her something and touching her. I feel a sickness inside of me. It's in my chest and digging downward. I look the woman in the eyes and she's someone else, someone I know, but maybe I don't. I'm still touching her, but she's gone and I'm surrounded by people staring at me. Their faces move in circles, jumping from body to body. The sky is black but it isn't night. There is no sky really. I'm smoking a joint or I'm taking some pills or I'm drinking a drink or I'm doing all of these things. The people are spinning and the walls are flying and that's okay. Walls can fly. My family is in the room and they're smoking my joint. Or they're taking my pills. Or they're drinking my drink. Or they're doing all of these things. I feel bad for everything and everyone, but mostly for everything since everyone is a part of it. I start to feel a little insane and regretful. I shouldn't have done something, though I'm not sure what. I get a feeling it deals with me existing. Someone says something that I don't understand and I'm lying dizzy on the floor. It's today.

STUFF MADE OF THINGS

Five days a week I sit in the gray seat of my red car from nineteen-ninety-something. I drive to a building where I do pointless things for eight hours with a half hour break somewhere in the middle. During this drive I either think nothing at all and end up at work surprised because I don't remember driving there, or I think meaningless, disconnected, often cynical thoughts until I end up at work surprised because I don't remember driving there.

Today is Saturday. I'm again driving to work. Normally I have the weekends off, but since I drank last night it just so happens that I have to go in. My stomach feels like hell. My head feels too heavy. There's a taste in my mouth that taste like death.

The sky is a bright white that eats away at everything it touches. It swallows up any hint of anything today may bring. I'm living in a world full of nothing. I wonder to myself if I care about it or not.

I arrive at work, turn off the car, and feel surprised because I don't remember driving here. I'm staring foreword at the large gray wall of the building in which I work. Dust floats by my face. I watch as I breathe it in. Everything today will be compresses itself into a tiny ball of nausea, which sits inside my stomach.

I almost feel sad.

I work at a store that specializes in selling stuff.

It doesn't really matter what it is.

There are commercials on TV for the place that I work. They usually show a family who's happy because they're surrounded by stuff that they bought for cheap from the place that I work. They wouldn't be happy if they didn't have the stuff, because the stuff is who they are. They wouldn't even be happy if they had bought it from someplace else, because they would've spent more money than the stuff was really worth.

My job is to open boxes. My job is to stack things. My job is to do nothing worth doing.

I'm standing in the backroom, holding a box knife in my hand. A large brown cardboard box is sitting at my feet. I'm supposed to open the box and take the stuff inside of it out. Instead I'm standing completely still, box knife in hand, staring at nothing in particular and thinking about nothing at all.

I feel sick.

I hear footsteps coming towards me, which wakes me up to the moment and I pretend to be working. My hands are pulling things out of the box.

I feel even more nauseous.

The footsteps fade away along with my attention to the work at hand. My mind is set on my stomach, which is getting worse. I go to the restroom in hopes of puking out whatever it is that's killing me. Instead of throwing up I just sit on the toilet and fall asleep.

I wake up and I'm pretty sure it's been about ten minutes. I wipe my ass even though I haven't shit, and I feel angry at everything.

Everything is awful.

I look in the mirror and notice my skin looks slightly gray. My head feels like it doesn't exist and my body feels like its slowly spinning.

I stand alone, staring ay myself in the mirror. Another ten minutes passes, before I make myself move.

It's two thirty in the afternoon. I've been working to take my mind off feeling like hell. My nausea has begun to subside, along with my headache. All that remains is a vague sense of something wrong with my body and my thoughts. The odd emptiness in my head is still there. A weakness in my muscles keeps me from doing much of anything. My eyes constantly try to close.

I've just opened a big box of stuff. Lots of little red things wait to be neatly stacked on a shelf. I'm standing in the middle of the aisle for little red things, slightly slumped over, stacking them where they go. I work as slow as possible, feeling somewhat comfortable in the aisle for little red things. All around me I see red. Above and below me is a dull and dirty white. My eyes are struggling to stay open as I stand staring at the little red things surrounding me. Between eternal blackness I view the world, a world of little red things.

Edges start to blur, so I make new ones.

I feel a little bit crazy which makes me feel a little less crazy. I tell myself to stop thinking about little red things and to start working again.

One of my coworkers appears out of nowhere, his hair a mess and his shirt stained. No one cares here on a Saturday. No one cares anytime really, but on weekends you can let it show.

"Hey," he says, "I was gonna take my break now. That cool?"

"Sure," I reply.

I don't care.

A little dark haired girl wearing a bright orange dress walks by. She knocks a big green thing off the shelf behind my coworker. He doesn't seem to notice as he continues to stare at me.

I feel myself colliding into everything, into myself, in a strange sensation. It's a familiar sensation. My world of little red things, which I'm not supposed to think about anymore, feels as if it's existed forever with me in the middle of it. I've just become what I've been before. Déjà vu is what I suppose I should call it. It feels more real than anything I've ever felt, yet my body, my mind, everything I am feels weak. My coworker has left and I'm alone again. The feeling is still there and I'm confused. It's as if I'm stuck in this moment, this life. I stand staring at nothing, thinking about now and what I'm feeling. I don't know how long it lasts. There isn't any sense of time.

The moment is gone and distant to me, just as it felt when I sat outside. I'm standing in the back with a box knife in hand again. I think of déjà vu and wonder what it could be. Is it really experiencing something I've done before? Somewhere I've been before? Not in the mundane sense, but in the sense that every single thing within that moment, the time, the place, the thoughts, the atoms, the reality of it all, has existed before. Is it all just one big circle we live over and over again?

Maybe it's just the brain fucking up.

I start to think about it too much and begin to stop making any sense.

My mind feels bored and I watch as it makes up things to entertain itself. I realize I forgot the déjà vu and then I forget I forgot the déjà vu. I decide it's time to go home even though I still have some work left to do.

I leave, drive home, and climb the stairs to my apartment, which is on the second floor of a two-story building.

The sun is setting, but clouds cover up the sky. A shallow, depressing blue shines in through the windows. I eat anything I can find that doesn't need cooked. My stomach feels like shit again, and I decide I need a cigarette. Standing on my balcony, smoking, I try not to think, but my body keeps yelling at me.

I need to sleep.

Ashley calls me before I go to bed. She tells me things about today. She'll be back tomorrow. I tell her I love her.

I fall asleep.

SUNDAY

I'm not alone. Ashley has come over after her trip to the place she's from. We sit and talk about what she did and whom she saw. She tells me about the day she woke up and no one was home, so she baked brownies and ate half of them then threw the other half away because they really didn't taste that good. When her brother came home he said it smelled like brownies. She pretended not know why.

I tell her about the party and the déjà vu I had before it. She didn't seem to have much to say about it. I didn't tell her about how it happened at work too. Not because I was hiding it. I just didn't feel like talking anymore. I talk to Ashley more than I talk to anyone else, but it's still barely at all. When we have a conversation, she's the one usually talking as I listen or half-listen or just pretend to listen.

I make pancakes that really don't taste that good.

We eat half of them.

"I wish we could discover telepathy," I tell her. I don't know why I'm thinking about telepathy. I don't know why I think about anything. I drink the cup of coffee that somehow ended up in front of me.

"I think we can," she says.

"I'm done with words," I say, "It's time we let them go. It's time we let everything go."

"People might not like what they see in other people's thoughts"

She takes a drink from her coffee.

"Would you see it?" I ask, "I think it would be more like feeling it."

"I was just saying it that way to get a point across," she says.

She looks away.

"I know," I say.

She's staring out the window. Her hair is pulled back and I can see her eyes as they gaze at nothing in particular which means she's thinking about something in particular.

"I'm sorry," I tell her, "I wish I could telepathize that to you."

"I bet it's the next step in evolution," she says not appearing to care.

"Telepathy?"

"Yea. I mean, we can get stronger and we can live longer, but that wouldn't make life any better. We need to know we're not alone. What's the point if we're alone?"

"No matter what happens, if you exist, you're alone. At least it seems that way."

"Maybe that would change."

"Maybe."

We stare at each other. I can tell what she's doing and I can tell she knows what I'm doing.

We're still alone.

"We tried," I say.

"I think it worked," she says, "We both knew what we we're trying to do."

"Kinda, but not really."

She smiles, or does something similar to a smile.

"What do you want to do today?" I ask.

"I don't care," she answers, "What do you want?"

"I don't care either," I say before drinking my coffee.

I do care, but I don't know what it is that I want, so I settle with not caring.

"Let's make something," she says.

"Let's make nothing," I say back.

"Let's do both at the same time."

"Let's do neither."

We go back to bed.

I'm not alone.

AGAIN

Nothing in particular happens.
Days go by and I watch as I live.
Or maybe I don't.
It doesn't really matter.
I work.
I work.
I work.

DEAD LEAVES

Something beautiful happened and I missed it.
I'm not sure what it was.
I just know that I missed it.
It happened while I was at work, which is when beautiful things always happen. I'm staring at walls and I'm opening boxes and I'm doing useless things with useless stuff, while somewhere else something beautiful is happening.

I'm calling in sick. A pathetic acting job over the phone and the rest of the day is mine.
Now I'm staring at the sunlight as it pours through the blankets that cover my face. I breathe in the air that's just left my lungs.
Maybe there's nothing beautiful.
I fall back asleep.

I wake up, get dressed, and leave. In between waking up and getting dressed I lay on the floor in my underwear staring at the sky and the corner of the tree out my window, while thinking about getting up to do something. In between getting dressed and leaving I stood in my living room and did nothing for quite a while.
I don't have a plan for today. I don't ever have a plan for anything really. All I ever have are vague goals with vague ideas of how to get there. All I want for today is to experience something beautiful. My detachment to life is collapsing away into a listless depression. I'm no longer just watching. I'm fading into a half existent being stuck partially in this world and partially in my mind.
I'm a ghost.
It's not some enlightened escape from life. It's a painful repulsion from feeling anything at all and at the same time an aching for any sign of meaning. It's being

stuck in a pointless story about a person whom you don't give a damn about, but deep down really want to.

I need something. I hate that I need something.

I feel a bit too melancholic.

I feel a bit too insincere.

One moment I'm distancing myself from life and the next I'm reaching out for any sign of being alive. It's a shaking in my mind over what the hell I want. Or what the hell I don't want. Both questions seem to have the same answer.

Nothing.

Or something.

It doesn't matter.

They're both the same thing.

It's October. I'm outside. I'm walking.

The world is blue and yellow and red and brown and orange. I go nowhere in particular, walking down streets I've walked before. The sidewalks are dark and wet from rain, which apparently happened earlier this morning, though no signs are left in the sky.

It all feels empty. I feel empty.

I've been here too long. In the past I used to think I'd be somewhere different, somewhere amazing, by now. I imagined I would be successful and I denied that I was dreaming the dreams of the average person. This was different. I was different.

But here I am, where I was, not somewhere else.

I walk and think nothing.

I need to think something.

I end up at someone's house and they give me a way to think. I burn it alone.

Sounds float around and into my head. I hear the drone of distant cars and the wavering of wind as it moves through everything. I feel myself becoming more and more aware of what's around me. Is it real awareness? Or is it falling deeper into a dream? The question is pointless. Everything could always be a dream.

My feet sit damp in dead leaves.
I feel sad, or something.
Maybe happy.
Maybe both.
The sunlight dances with the shadows of the shaking leaves left in the trees. I stare at the ground and it looks too real to exist. I try to decide what that means, but come up with nothing. Sounds keep floating around and into my head as I sit within this amplified existence.
I'm alone.
I laugh.
I think too much.

I'm moving again. I began to feel uneasy sitting in the same spot. Paranoia, or something. Now I'm watching my feet as they move without me telling them to. I feel separate. I feel unreal. I smoke a cigarette and it burns my lungs.
For some reason I enjoy it.
The sidewalk takes me to a place I've been before. I'm staring into an empty building. Or maybe it's full of nothing. I'm gazing at its windows, watching the reflection of myself and the street behind me. A cloud floats by that covers the sun as the world becomes enveloped in its bluish-gray shadow.
Time begins to slow, or at least my perception of it does. A car drives by. It's a red car. And a man walks by dressed in a long tan jacket, the kind no one wears anymore.
It all happens, now.
Time speeds up again. It speeds up past what it was before. I feel it all too much. I feel sick. There's a pain in my stomach. It burns and it stabs and it cuts. I've felt this pain before.
Faster.
Burning. Stabbing. Cutting. Everything.
It all snaps into place.
I'm standing in eternity again. Déjà vu? It's like before, but even stronger. I've always stood in front of this

empty building, with its empty reflection of an empty self. The sickness in my stomach has always been there and always will be. The thought of it makes me even more nauseous, but I can't throw up. I'm too caught in what's happening around me. The colors and the sounds and the smells take over my life as my thoughts disappear.

It's a familiar confusion.

Everything.

Time slows down to what feels like something normal. The sun has returned. I feel its warmth on my skin and the nausea in my stomach begins to fade. The sensation, the déjà vu, is still there though. It's not going away. Everything around me still feels strangely too familiar. It's not that I've been here before. It's that I've always been here. I've never left and I'll never leave. Time doesn't exist, even though I can sense what I thought it to be. There is no past and there is no future. There's not even a now. Nothing exists. A nothing made of something. Or a something made of nothing. It's just a motion.

An endless collision.

My thoughts don't make any sense, so I give up on thinking. All I can do is watch. I'm sitting on a bench next to the building I was just at. This sensation is staying with me.

Am I going crazy?

The thought keeps crossing my mind and I can't answer it. I can't stop thinking even though I'd like to. People walk pass me and they seem like characters in a movie, completely fake yet with a meaning behind every movement they make. It doesn't make sense. When I look closer, all of reality seems this way.

Everything is fake, yet everything is real.

No. It's all useless words in my head.

It doesn't make any sense.

I sit staring at all that happens.

I have to move.

I walk and think something.

I need to think nothing.

I end up at a restaurant not far from where I was. Half cooked pancakes and coffee sit in front of me. It's a mistake being here. Dealing with others is nearly impossible right now. When the waitress arrived I just stared at the way her hands moved as she was saying things. When I realized she was talking to me I apparently uttered pancakes and coffee, seeing as that's what's in front of me.

My sight has been occupied on each person here for far too long. I watch them talking, eating, existing. I've watched them talk and eat and exist for all eternity.

No, there isn't even eternity.

Just useless words in my head.

There's an overweight man in the booth next to me. He's eating with an overweight woman, presumably his wife. They keep talking about someone they know and how that someone they know is messing up his life. They eat their bacon and eggs and talk at the same time.

In the far corner is an old man in a dirty blue work shirt. He's drinking coffee and reading the newspaper and talking to himself. He looks like he's been working since the day that he was born, but at the same time he's the laziest fuck on earth.

I feel bad for being an asshole.

I'm always an asshole.

Some song by someone is playing in the restaurant. The blown out speakers above my head painfully thud out a drum beat while fuzzy guitars play alongside them. A man's voice crackles in and out, singing words I can't understand.

It moves me to feel sad even though it's awful. I haven't felt this way in a long time. I'm not sure I've ever felt this way actually. I become attached to the feeling I get as it pulls me deep down into my life.

What am I doing here?

I stare at the ceiling and think about forever. Small bits of cobwebs hanging between the cracks of the ceiling slightly flutter from the fans blowing across the room. I watch them move back and forth without ever really moving at all.

My waitress returns and asks me something and I say something back. She kept digging for an object in her pocket, but I couldn't tell what because she never seemed to get ahold of it.

I decide to not be an asshole anymore.

I've always decided this though. I've always sat here feeling strange and thinking I'm an asshole.

I sit and drink my coffee and eat my half cooked pancakes. The sun shines in through the window in front of me. It's light bounces through the blinds and falls into my eyes.

I feel happy. I feel strange. I feel happy.

I've always been happy, or at least I've always been happy here, which is where I've always been. But I know that I haven't always been here, because I remember not being here and I remember not being happy. The sensation, this situation, confuses and overwhelms me.

This déjà vu, or something, is bringing me an awareness that wasn't there before. My entire life I thought I was always present for, always watching everything that happened. But now I'm not so sure. Now I feel like I can really see what is happening. I can see the way that nothing ever changes, yet never stays the same. I don't really understand it, but I'm aware of it.

It's just a motion, and here it collides.

My thoughts are becoming hectic and confused. My happiness is gone, but it's not replaced by sadness. I feel more tired than anything. I want to stop thinking, but I can't. I'm too aware, especially of my own thoughts and how they don't even seem to be mine. I don't control them. But I can't deny that they're everything that I am. Am I everything but myself?

There's a constant question in my head, about what I don't know. Along with it are constant answers that make no sense.

Nothing makes sense.

I pay for my coffee and half cooked pancakes and leave.

The sun is gone. Hints of its light remain, shining blue on the clouds left hanging in the dark sky.

I walk fast.

The sight of concrete below my feet.

Streetlight.

The smell of damp and dying trees.

Streetlight.

The sound of a cars driving past.

Streetlight.

The feeling of cold wind on my face.

Streetlight.

A lonely, empty nothing.

Streetlight.

Nothing.

Streetlight.

Nothing.

The door to my apartment.

The stairway smells like cigarettes and old carpet. It's a familiar smell, even without the déjà vu.

I'm in bed.

What?

I can't come up with more.

I fall asleep.

FOREVER

I wake up in the middle of the night. Even the pitch-black room looks too familiar. I feel sad and lie without moving. Emotions cut through me like they haven't in a long time. Something has changed within me. Am I even still myself? The nothingness I believed myself to be me has been replaced with something indescribable. I'm no longer stuck between the emptiness and the everything. I have become the entirety of both.

Am I going insane?

These thoughts that enter my mind don't make any sense. Yet they do. I must be crazy if they do. How long will I be this way?

It really hits me that I'm stuck in a state of déjà vu.

An empty mood falls over me. Before, thoughts were piling upon themselves, creating chaos in my mind. Now there is nothing. I feel broken, lying alone staring at the dark.

I always have.

Nothing happens.
Nothing.
The sun rises as I fall back asleep.

THIS IS WHERE YOU ARE

Water.
The sky is every color.
The ocean.
Silent music in my ear.
A tree dances up from the sea.
Into the sky.
Everything is perfect.
"This is where you are."
No.
I'm somewhere else.
Fire.
I'm surrounded.
Fire.
I'm somewhere else.
People.
I'm surrounded.
People.
"This is where you are."
I want to go back.
"This is where you are."
But I've been here before.
"This is where you are."
Everything is awful.
"This is where you are."
This is where I am.
People.
I'm surrounded.
The sky is white.
The ocean.
I'm awake.

TALK

I wake up around two in the afternoon. My phone is ringing. I've heard it before.

It's Ashley.

She's coming over.

She's here.

I answer the door.

"You look like hell," she says.

"Thanks," I reply.

Her eyes scream at me. They scream familiar, like everything else.

She sits around while I clean myself up.

I stand in the shower for too long, letting the water fall over me again and again.

Now I'm staring in the mirror. I'm staring at myself, talking without saying a thing.

What the fuck is going on with me?

She's sitting at the kitchen table.

I'm sitting next to her.

"I'm having a déjà vu."

"Really?"

"Yea."

She looks me in the eyes. The experience pulses and I feel a bit sick.

"Yea," I say again.

She stands up to get a drink.

"It hasn't stopped," I tell her.

"Since last time? Didn't you have one awhile back? You can't have a déjà vu that long," she says.

"Since yesterday. It started yesterday."

She's drinking a soda, or something. She doesn't seem to care. Maybe she does. But she doesn't seem to.

"I don't think they last that long," she says.

"They don't," I say.

"Then maybe your just crazy."

"Yea," I mumble back.

"I wasn't serious. You're not crazy," she says, stressing the not.

I stare at the refrigerator. It stares back at me.

"I think I might be," I tell her.

She rolls her eyes and walks into the other room. I sit alone for a minute then get up and join her. It's raining outside and the windows are open. It's cold.

"It's cold," I say.

"Then shut the windows," she replies.

I leave them open.

"So déjà vu?" she asks.

I slowly nod yes while staring out the window. Dark trees, wet from the rain, sit outside. Most of their leaves are gone. The scene sits within my mind and exist forever like everything else that I experience.

"Hey," she says, "You're fine. They say young people have them all the time. It happens less and less the older you get. It's your brain changing, I think. A misfire in there somewhere. I don't know much about them. I've only gotten them a few times. They never seem to last more than a few seconds though. Are you sure it's déjà vu?"

"Yea," I say.

She says something to me but I don't listen.

I'm stuck staring at the wet trees. I've sat here and experienced this before. I know I have. Ashley moves closer to me. She pulls my face around towards her, looks me in the eyes and says nothing. Her face looks so known to me it's no longer hers but my own. Everything around me is a part of myself.

It's all too much.

She kisses me. She tries to make me feel better.

She doesn't.

I half smile to make her feel better.

"I'm fine," I tell her.

"Tell me about it," she says, "the déjà vu."

"I'm not sure how much I could say."

"Well it's like you've done something before, right?"

"Yea, I guess. It's like I've been here before. But it's more than that. It's not a feeling of having done something. I have done these things before, but not in the past. I've always been doing them, now. It doesn't make sense when I say it, but it's like there is no past to have experienced. There's no future either. There's only this endless sort of now, and I can feel it."

She looks confused. Or she looks deep in thought. Probably both. Or neither. I look back out the window. She says something about life and memories and time and me being okay and how people have weird experiences like this all the time. I didn't really listen to what she said. I was busy watching the rain drip down the black, damp bark of the tree outside. I turn to her and nod to what she told me. She smiles.

The rest of the day happens while I watch it unfold within itself. I feel as if I'm on the edge of understanding something, yet also on the edge of falling forever into ignorance. I balance upon thin, hollow lines within my mind, looking down into the possibilities of what may happen to me. Standing upon this emptiness, I become no more than what I already am.

BEFORE

I've done this forever.

Nothing.

A sickness sits in my stomach.

I'm staring at people as they shop at the place that I work. I can't stand it anymore, so I go outside for a smoke. It's cold, but I don't care. I want to be alone. This sensation that's taken over my life, the déjà vu, has made me more aware of everything that I experience. It's as if reality has been amplified through itself, through its endlessness.

I hesitate to call it reality though.

It's just an experience.

Is that what makes something real?

Endless questions clutter my mind. None of them ever have any answers. Somehow I can still manage to be around other people even though I'm strangely stuck within these questions and this déjà vu.

Somehow I can still seem normal. Maybe its because I've always been disconnected from everyone. I'm expected to be reclusive.

In the distance I can hear people talking.

I go back to work.

My stomach feels awful as I get through the day. The sickness makes me think about dying, while this déjà vu makes me question whether or not I'll actually die. For a moment I fear both death and life. For a moment I fear everything. I sink into an apathy, which makes the fear fade. I have to force myself to work, although I don't really get anything done. I just make myself seem busy. Small instances with no real significance capture my attention and throw me even deeper into my mind.

The sound of water dripping.

The smell of an empty room.

The sight of a door left slightly open.

I watch the clock as time passes, which it never really does.

Somehow I finish work and leave behind today.

BEING SOMETHING

It's two days after Halloween and I'm at a Halloween party. I'm a zombie, both in life and in costume.

I'm a zombie every Halloween.

The déjà vu, which started a week ago and hasn't left since, has broken me down into a reclusive mess. Even more than before, I sit inside myself watching everything that happens. Yet I'm no longer separate from what I experience. What lies inside myself is now the same as what exists outside of my mind. The sensation of existing in these moments forever has sewn me into place within this life.

"I hate this song," Ashley says to me. She's a vampire. She's a vampire every Halloween.

"Me too," I tell her. I've never heard the song before, but I already know I hate it too.

I take a drink.

We're sitting alone on a couch in the corner of the room. People are all around us. I know most of them, but a few I don't recognize. Friends of friends, or something.

A man dressed up as Jesus sits down next to us and says nothing. I turn to him and he looks at me and laughs.

Another song comes on.

"I hate this song," I tell Ashley.

"Me too," she replies.

I take a drink.

I'm standing on the patio, smoking a cigarette. My friend is with me, telling me about something. I don't really listen. When he's done talking I tell him something. I don't really listen to what I say either.

The déjà vu has been moving around my mind all night. Everything that happens feels as if it's been done. Some moments feel more familiar than others. The sensation wavers in and out at random.

My friend borrows a cigarette from me.

"So you're still in school?" I ask.

"Yea," he says, "I can't quit. I've got nothing if I do."

I've got nothing.

My friend goes inside and I'm alone.

I keep drinking until the bottle is empty and then head back inside. People are standing around talking about something I don't understand. A show on TV, or something. They talk about things that never really happened and people that don't really exist, although they talk as if they really did happen and really do exist.

I feel cynical and walk away.

Someone dressed up in a costume that doesn't make any sense is standing next to me.

"What are you?" I ask, surprised I said anything at all.

"I'm everything," she says.

I nod and fake a laugh.

"I'm guessing you're the undead?" she asks me.

I nod and fake a laugh.

I can't come up with anything to say so we stand in silence until she walks away to talk to someone else.

I stand alone drinking.

The shitty music that was playing still sounds awful, but I'm drunk enough to dance to it. Ashley is sitting on the couch watching me. I laugh as I turn towards her. She laughs back. I feel depressed with myself and stop dancing.

I'm on the couch next to her.

"Why'd you stop?" she asks.

"I felt dumb."

"Why?"

"It's a bad song."

"Yea," she says, "But that doesn't matter."

I think to myself that nothing does and I feel more depressed. I take a drink that last forever.

My friend sits down next to me. He's now dressed in blue tights, a blue shirt, and blue face paint.

"I'm the color blue," he tells me.

I laugh.

"You wanna go smoke?" he asks.

"Yea. I do," I reply.

I turn to tell Ashley I'll be right back.

She gives me a stare that means too much for me to understand right now.

"Don't be stupid," she tells me.

"I won't."

She stares me in the eyes.

"Do what you want," she tells me as she turns away.

I know that I'm already in trouble, so I leave.

I'm sitting in my friend's car getting stoned and listening to music I've heard before, but don't know when or where. I'm already half drunk and smoking is probably a bad idea, but I don't care. I can feel myself getting more and more fucked up. The déjà vu is getting stronger too. The music moves through me and leaves me feeling full of life.

I feel good. I feel really good. I keep smoking. I keep feeling good.

I look to my right and the color blue is sitting next to me. I laugh. The color blue laughs. My head is moving. My mind is moving. I keep smoking.

I close my eyes and I'm caught in the sound of an eternity that's gathered into one single moment. I feel nothing but the sound that enters my ears.

I look to my right and the color blue is gone. I'm not even in the car anymore. I'm walking back into the party. I begin to feel paranoid because I don't remember moving.

I feel confused.

I forget the paranoia.

I feel good.

I'm looking for Ashley but I can't find her.

She finds me.

"I was watching you look for me," she says, " I was right next to you."

I laugh.

She rolls her eyes and walks away.

People move past me as I move past them. The music that was playing has gotten louder. I'm not sure if it's because I'm stoned or someone has turned it up. Either way I'm feeling fine as I float around the house not talking to anyone.

A feel a pulse of the sensation in my mind. I feel everything falling into place. I'm no longer confused. Instead, I'm becoming too aware of what's going on, too aware for being drunk and stoned. My body feels intensely existent. The people around me seem empty and fake.

I see the lives behind everyone.

I see our pointlessness.

Are we nothing?

I drink.

I fucking drink forever, now.

What else is there to do?

I laugh too myself, or at myself.

These thoughts are too much for me. I feel crazy and alone in the middle of everyone. My heart is pounding and I can feel myself coming into existence with each pulse of blood through my body.

Jesus, or the man dressed like him, is standing next to me laughing too, which makes me laugh even more. I feel more and more like something is wrong with me. My head feels empty. It's moving back and forth, not to the music, but to some nothingness in my mind that tells it to fall around. I feel sick and step outside.

A girl with a pumpkin mask and a witch hat on is sitting next to me. We don't say anything. I'm smoking a cigarette and feeling like I'm killing myself. I smoke half of the cigarette before throwing it out. I stare at the distant streetlights as they shoot halos of amber colored light into my eyes. For just a moment, I feel happy. It's like a glimpse into some sort of possibility for my life. It shoots through me and disappears within a single moment, leaving me feeling worse than before.

I turn towards the girl, but she's gone.

I'm alone.

I'm confused.

I'm dizzy.

The party goes on in a blur.

I'm coming down from being stoned. Now I'm just a drunk mess falling onto the couch. My stomach is killing me. Ashley sits down next to me.

"I told you," she says.

"You didn't tell me anything," I say back.

She shakes her head and brushes my hair.

I'm drunk. I take a drink. It makes me feel sick and I decide I can't drink anymore. I feel depressed. I feel like I'm ruining my life. I can't enjoy anything. I fuck myself up. I fuck everything up.

The ceiling is spinning.

"You don't fuck everything up," Ashley says.

I didn't realize I said it out loud.

"Yes I do," I say.

"No. You just act stupid sometimes."

"Yea."

The ceiling is still spinning and I feel myself lying there spinning forever. I don't want to be here forever. I don't want to be anywhere forever, but especially not here. Not with myself like this.

I'm in the bathroom puking. I guess I'm still stoned because I'm sitting in the bathroom puking and I feel like everyone else has stopped existing and I have to spend the rest of forever in this shitty little bathroom listening to an endless shitty party happening outside the door. There's a little plush grim reaper hanging from the light. I stare at it and laugh at myself. I puke again. Fucking again.

I'm in the car and Ashley is driving us home. Lights fly pass the window. Each one makes me feel worse.

"I'm never drinking again," I tell her.

"You say that every time," she says.

I stare at my feet and watch them spin. Fucking again.

"Yea, I do," I say.

We're at home, in bed. She takes my shoes off and I feel pathetic.

"Fuck," I say.

"Yea," she says.

I fall asleep.

I wake up in the middle of the night to take a piss. My head is pounding.

I feel awful. I feel dead.

I look in the mirror and I'm still dressed up like a zombie. I don't laugh. I don't do anything. I stand there.

I stand there and feel like shit.

I go back to bed.

AGAIN, AGAIN

It's November.

I'm sitting in my car.

I feel a sick knot in my stomach.

Again. Fucking again.

It takes a while for me to gather the strength to get out of my car and walk into the building where I work.

Again.

I'm standing next to a box.

Again.

I work for a while, until I look up at the clock and realize it's been half an hour. After which I stop working and walk around the store looking busy.

The déjà vu still remains. It vibrates in and out in strength, but never leaves. At some points it lingers in my mind, slightly covering everything in the sensation of having experienced what is being experienced. At other times it takes over my life and thrust me into a state of pure awareness of the present and it's endlessness.

Again. Fucking again.

I'm standing next to a box.

It takes a while for me to gather the strength to open the box and take the stuff inside of it out, instead of just staring at the wall and thinking nothing.

I work for a while, until I look up at the clock and realize it's time for my break. I stop and go sit outside.

A bag of chips and a shitty sandwich.

Again.

At least the sun is out.

I smoke a cigarette and read a book about something.

I think about what I want my life to be.

I come up with nothing more than what I don't want it to be, which is this.

Back to work.

Again.

I'm standing next to a box.

Fucking again.

I'm standing next to a box.

Again.

The knot in my stomach is burning. I feel myself fall into the sensation of the now that last forever, and my damn stomach is killing me.

Burning. Stabbing. Cutting.

Again. Fucking again.

I work.

Burning. Stabbing. Cutting.

It's time to leave.

Again.

The pain is fading.

I go home.

Ashley is there.

We watch a movie I've seen before.

We sleep together.

Again.

NOTHING

Most of the time I'm in a daze.

Most of the time I'm at work.

I stand around thinking about nothing but the pain in my stomach, which is growing worse everyday, and how for all eternity I'll stand there at work doing nothing and feeling like shit.

I went to the doctor over the pain. He gave me some pills that did nothing. I went back and he gave me some more pills that did nothing. I went back again and he said I should take some tests. Give him lots of money to look at me, or something. I told him I wasn't coming back. I went home and drank beer until I passed out in my front room listening to music that made me feel cool for being pissed off. I woke up in the morning laughing at myself, feeling sad and alone.

The sensation that's become my life, the déjà vu, gets stronger everyday. Some days I'm lucky to function. I no longer question if I'm going crazy.

Either I have gone crazy, or existence itself has.

Either way everything is fucked.

It's Sunday.

It's nothing.

Ashley is here.

I've kept everything about my life since the déjà vu to myself. Ashley knows more about me than anyone, yet really she knows nothing. I told her that I still feel it, the déjà vu, but she either doesn't understand how much I do or I didn't really let her know. To everyone I seem like a normal, depressed, twenty something.

My life is pathetically falling apart. My job sucks, but what job doesn't? I have a place to live, food to eat, people who love me. I ruin the days by smoking and drinking and feeling bad for myself. I constantly feel like something is missing, though I can't say what.

I should stop smoking. I should stop drinking.

But I don't.

I tell myself I will. And for a few days I do. But my stomach still feels bad, and the déjà vu still yells through every monotonous thing that I do.

So I smoke more and I drink more.

Something has to change.

But when you're stuck in one place in time, nothing changes. Things just move around.

It's all still there.

It's all still here.

It always will be.

Ashley is sitting next to me. Some movie about something is playing on the television. I look out the window.

"It's snowing," I tell her.

She doesn't react for a few seconds, then turns her head towards the window.

"Really?" she asks.

"Yeah."

"Oh."

She turns back to the movie.

I forget the pointless interaction we just had and stare back out of the window. Snow falls in quick white drifts through the halo of a streetlight in the distance.

I want more than this.

I want to lose myself.

But I can't.

I step outside to smoke a cigarette, just to feel anything at all besides the oppressive thoughts that float throughout my apartment.

The ground is wet from dead snowflakes. White specks float pass my eyes and melt as soon as they land upon the earth. It's not yet cold enough for them to stay alive.

I smoke my cigarette and stare at the dying snowflakes and the dead trees and the empty, cold sky. I feel surrounded by death. This moment rings throughout me. I see the déjà vu, this feeling of eternity, for what it really is.

It's death.

It's life.

It's both at the same time.

The feeling I get overpowers me and I begin to feel sick. A weakness in my legs creeps upwards and takes over my head. I look up at the snow falling into my eyes and begin to feel dizzy. Black limbs and a glowing night sky spin around in my vision. Specks of white fly into my eyes.

I throw up red onto the ground.

Burning. Stabbing. Cutting.

I feel calm standing above my bright red vomit in the cold air.

I'm dying.

THE SHAPES OF SELF

I'm no longer human. I'm not sure I'm even alive. Although I must be if I'm here. Limbs move past my vision. Tree limbs. My limbs? I can't feel a thing.

Limbs move past my vision. Tree limbs? My limbs. I can hear a ringing in my right ear. It's getting louder.
I'm no longer. I'm not sure. I must be.

It's bright and colorful and I want it. When I touch it I lose myself. Limb by limb I fall apart.

Limbs move past. My limbs? Tree limbs. I feel everything. I can hear a ringing in my right ear. It's getting louder.

It's bright and colorful and I want it. I don't touch it. I want it. Limb by limb I fall apart. My limbs?
I'm no longer.

I can hear them. Myself. Becoming. I must be. A ringing in my right ear. Limbs.

It's bright and colorful and I want it. I fucking want it but I don't touch it. I'll never touch it. Ringing. Limbs. Myself.

I'm no longer. I must be. I'm not sure. Limb by limb I fall apart. My limbs? Tree limbs? My limbs.
Damnit. Damnit. Damnit.

Limb by limb I fall apart.

I'm no longer human.

A ringing in my right ear and I'm awake.

SCRAPER

Winter wraps its arms around me as I sit alone in my car from nineteen-ninety something, waiting for its engine to come alive. Snow has piled upon the windows, so I'm hidden within my own little world of cold and cheap automobile interior. The cigarette burning in my mouth is the only heat I have.

My life, the déjà vu, the pain in my stomach, everything, has been dulled by winter's cold presence. For a while I was sure I was going to die, and I almost looked forward to it. The pain however faded, and now I live with a dull ache that lives deep inside of me, both in my body and mind. I float like the snowflakes though every day of my life, heading for my fate of melting into eternity.

Into nothing.

I turn the radio on and listen to bad music until I change the station to static. I sit listening to the noise, feeling the painful cold air surrounding my body.

The car is alive.

I drive to work.
I work.
I drive home.

Ashley isn't here. She's back in her hometown somewhere. I'm alone. I'm glad I'm alone. All I want to do is lie on the floor and stare at the ceiling, smoking pot and listening to music.

No.

What I really want is something else. I don't know what it is. I just know it's not this.

Not this.

But this is what I have.

I accept it and leave it behind, drifting further away into my mind. I live in my thoughts. No. I live in thoughts. They're not mine. No. Fuck it. I don't live at all.

I'm lying in the hallway, listening to sad acoustic music and thinking about other people. The small hallway is brightly lit and white, as I lie staring at its empty walls and ceiling.

There's nothing here.

I'm high and feeling sad.

I feel sad about the people I've lost. I feel sad about the people I still have in my life. I feel sad about everyone. I feel sad about myself.

I miss a life I know I never lived.

The déjà vu lingers on the edge of my mind, flowing through me with every hit I take. More and more I fall into myself and eternity. Why? I don't know. It just happens. I don't question it anymore. All I do anymore is feel shitty about myself and my life.

I'm high and lonely, lying in my hallway, staring at nothing and listening to sad acoustic music.

My life has crawled down to a miserable stop.

This needs to change. Everything needs to change. I stand up and walk into my living room. I'm really fucking high and moving to the sad sounding acoustic music.

What's the point? I can become who I want to be. I can live the life I want to live. In the end it doesn't matter though. It all dies, like all the people I know someday will die. There's no difference between an awful life and a good one. There is no point.

This thought thrashes my mind as I move around my apartment staring at the things I own. Objects of my past make me feel a yearning for a more human life. I want to feel love again. I want to feel happy, but my mind doesn't let me. It yells at me about the pointlessness of it all. Why the fuck does it matter? I feel caught in the middle of nowhere with no escape. I'm falling through emptiness with no meaning in sight. I feel a fear burning deep inside of me.

I think about it all and think about it all too much. I give up on myself and sit down in front of the TV. I put on an old black and white samurai flick to pass the time. It takes me ten minutes to figure out how to start the damn movie because I'm too stoned to figure out the remote control. It plays for a while and I fade off into my mind. I feel myself coming down halfway through and all I want right now is to not be my normal self, so I roll another joint and keep getting stoned. I watch as a group of samurai protect a worthless town full of pointless people and die saving the purposeless existence of life. Their actions move through me. They play through life's senselessness with their own given meaning. Their lives become everything as they die in empty beauty.

There isn't a point to any of this.

There is no meaning.

I have to give it meaning.

But why should I give it meaning?

Because there's nothing better to do?

It's a futile significance that dies along with myself.

Yet in this endless empty drifting, what else is there to do?

I wonder if I'm too stoned to be making any sense.

I feel empty again, but I don't let it stay.

I have to change.

I can't keep falling down through this depressing life.

I start to cry as I sit alone. I haven't cried in a long time and it feels good. I sit face to face with my futility in life and decide that I need to become something more than who I am.

I'm sitting in silence and listening too hard to nothing. I begin to feel crazy, which seems to happen more and more. A pain begins to grow in my stomach.

Burning. Stabbing. Cutting.

I need to change.

Burning. Stabbing. Cutting.

I need to.

Burning.

Stabbing.

Cutting.

I fall asleep.

HELLO

I'm playing hide and seek with David Bowie. He hides and I seek. He finds me hiding in a box and tells me that's not how to play hide and seek. I tell him to go to hell, then feel bad because I really like David Bowie and now he doesn't like me. My dad walks in and he looks like David Bowie too. I'm talking to David Bowie and my dad who looks like David Bowie, and we're standing in the middle of a crowd of people fighting. I can't remember which David Bowie is my dad so I decide David Bowie is my dad. I ask what the people are fighting about, but before I can get an answer everyone is gone. I'm playing hide and seek with no one. I hide and I seek. I find myself hiding in a box and tell myself that's not how to play hide and seek. I tell myself to go to hell, then feel bad because I really like myself and now I don't like myself. I'm talking to no one and I'm standing in the middle of nowhere. I can't remember what I was doing so I decide I wasn't doing anything. I ask myself what the point of doing nothing is, but before I can get an answer I'm doing something. I wake up tired.

MEMORY

It's Christmas Eve and I'm with my family. My life is in a strange state of confusion. I'm exploding within at the thought of changing everything about myself, but I haven't done a thing to bring it about. Everyday I still work, and every night I still pass the time depressed and slowly killing myself.

I know my family is worried about me. Every time I see them they ask me about what I want to do with my life. They suggest things that could make me happier, but really everything they suggest would just make me worse.

I'm sitting next to my mom who's sitting next to an old plastic Christmas tree. It shines its multicolored lights across the room, giving me the feeling of living within a fragment of a childhood memory.

My family life has fallen apart lately.

Most people are too busy with their own lives to be apart of someone else's. I no longer see distant relatives like I did when I was young. The few who will always be close to me are the only ones I see anymore.

"So have you finished your album yet?" my mom asks.

"Not yet," I reply while staring at a picture of my family posing in front of a place I don't recognize.

I haven't worked on my music in a long time.

Every time I try, nothing comes out. I have ideas in my head of what I want to create, yet when I try to make them happen all I get is a pathetic chunk of sound that doesn't resemble anything I wanted to make. I gave up on it a while ago, but I haven't told my family. When I dropped out of school I told them that I would become successful in my own way. I would be what I wanted to be.

I can't tell them that I've given up on myself.

I've tried writing too, but all I can get is a few pages before I decide it's all shit. I wish I could just tell my family that I don't know what I want to do. I don't know anything about myself. I wish I could tell them that that all I want to do is figure this life out. But I can't tell them that. I can't tell anyone any truths about myself.

Any thing true about myself is wordless.

Any truth at all is really.

"I'm writing too," I tell my mom just to make my situation sound better.

"Really? A book?"

"Kinda. Short stories. Maybe a book. I dunno. Work gets in the way."

She gets a worried look on her face, which I'm used to seeing. I turn and look at the Christmas tree. It's small and decorated in ornaments my siblings and I made growing up.

Popsicle sticks and felt and glitter and pictures of us as children.

I feel a bit sad.

"Well you know you can do anything Ferris," my mom tells me, "Just don't give up."

I give a smile that's half sincere and half just to comfort her. My brother and sister walk into the room, talking to each other and laughing.

My brother is the oldest of us. He lives just outside of town, working as driver for a company that delivers frozen meals to people's doorsteps. My sister attends grad school, studying economics, or something.

The two of them start talking about some of our messed up family members. My uncle just got arrested for selling pot to a fifteen year old. My seventeen-year-old cousin just dropped out of school and dates some thirty-year-old guy who works at a laundromat.

"Dad's still drunk all the time," my brother says, "He called me last week and I couldn't understand anything he was saying."

"Well at least we turned out alright," my sister jokes.

I laugh in my head.

"How's your album coming?" my sister asks me out of nowhere.

"Eh. It's okay. Kinda far from being done," I tell her.

"He's writing now," my mom says.

I begin to feel sick.

"A book?" my sister asks.

"Eh. Kinda. I'm just writing what I can," I say.

"Have you thought about going to school again? There's lots of good schools out there for writing," she tells me.

"I don't really want to go to school again," I reply.

My stomach begins to crawl up my chest.

"Leave him alone," my brother says, "I didn't go to school and I'm doing fine."

"I just don't want to see you regretting anything in the future," she tells me as she looks me in the eyes.

"I won't," I say as I get up to go to the bathroom.

I'm not throwing up. I'm just standing in front of the mirror looking at myself.

I look awful.

Dark circles sit below my eyes.

I've lost a lot of weight.

My skin is pale, almost gray.

No wonder my family worries about me.

I stand there for a while looking at myself and not really thinking much. I love my family, but the apathy that's covered my life has muted my feelings for everyone that I love.

I feel like shit for not being a better person.

I stare closely into the eyes in the mirror.

What are you doing?

I leave the bathroom.

My mom is sitting alone again. I sit down next to her. I feel like telling her the truth. Of everyone I know I feel like she needs to know more than anyone.

"I don't know what I want to do," I say.

She looks at me confused.

"What?" she asks.

"I don't know anything about my life," I say, "I want to be something, but I don't know what. Right now I just want to be nothing." I remember I'm talking to my mom, the person who cares about me more than anyone. I can't bring myself to say any more. To tell her the trouble that my life has become would be cruel.

I look up at her and give a half smile.

"But I'm not giving up," I say, "I wont."

She smiles back.

"I was serious when I said you could do anything," she tells me, "Life is hard. Trust me. I know. You're dad is proof of that. Just know that I love you. That lots of people love you."

I feel something. I can't say what. It's regret, desire, happiness, and sadness all mixed into one vague emotion. My déjà vu starts to kick in. It's been weakly drifting by for a while, but out of nowhere it grabs my mind and throws me into the present. I'm sitting, staring at my mother and feeling like I've sat here in this floral printed seat next to our multicolored Christmas tree for all of time.

"It's Christmas," my mom says to me, "So let's cheer up." She calls for my brother and sister. I feel the déjà vu pulsing through everything. Why now? I try to calm myself.

"Time for presents?" my sister asks.

My mom picks up a few wrapped boxes and hands them out to us. My sister opens something, then my brother opens something, then I open something. My sister lifts up her gift, a blue pair of fuzzy slippers.

"I needed these!" she exclaims.

"Whoa," my brother murmurs, "Déjà vu. I know this has happened before."

My sister and mother laugh it off while I explode in my mind at the thought of someone else having a déjà vu near me. Even if it was just the kind of déjà vu people often have, I felt as if maybe I wasn't alone. But I know that it wasn't the same as mine. I know that my brother is back within the normal way of living life.

Still, I can't let it go.

"I had one too," I tell him.

"Weird," he replies with a laugh.

Nothing else comes of it as my family continues on with Christmas without giving a second thought to the experience that secretly has taken over my life.

I feel shot back into myself.

We resume giving gifts until the night has reached its end. As I leave I tell my family I love them and they tell me the same.

I go home feeling more alone than I ever have.

THE DAY AFTER CHRISTMAS EVE

I sit around my apartment doing nothing all day. I call my father but I get no answer. I call Ashley and tell her that I love her. I sit and stare out of the window for an hour. I eat leftover food. I feel pathetic. I fall asleep thinking about the times that I was alive, even though I probably never was.

HUMAN

My father lives in a dirty white house surrounded by cornfields and dead grass. He lives with two other people, whom always seem to change whenever we visit. Last August, my brother and I drove the five hours it takes to see him. The sky burned white and the air was thick. The gravel driveway that led up to his house made the sound that only a car driving over gravel can make.

It made me feel sick of being where I was.

My father came out of the house as we parked the car. He wore tan shorts that didn't quite reach his knees, and a baby blue button up with vague stains along the right side. On his head was a trucker hat with a worn off logo for a company I didn't recognize. He gave me a hug and the smell of whiskey and canned meat entered my senses.

"Goddamn you're gettin old," he told me, taking off his hat and rubbing his shaggy gray hair.

Sounds of television poured out of the screen door as we sat on the porch and talked about whatever my father felt like talking about.

"Those mother fuckers down the road keep trying to borrow shit from us," he said angrily, "I know they ain't gonna give anything back if we let em. Every damn day they come by. They got a little boy with em, he's always looking like he's thinkin of stealin something."

I sat quietly and stared out at the field of dead grass along the house. My mind disappeared and the rest of the conversation vanished. Every time my father talks, my thoughts forcefully escape me. It's as if my body refuses to acknowledge were it came from.

The rest of the day happened in a blur, as my thoughts turned themselves away from the world around me. At one point my father tried to talk to me about what I was doing with my life.

"So you in a band now?" he asked.

"Eh," I replied reluctantly, "I just kind of make my own music."

"You watch that music," he said in a tone that showed he was thinking of his own life.

"Watch the music?" my brother asked.

My dad sat quiet for a minute then lifting his hat off of his head replied with a grunt. I wasn't sure what to make of it, so I decided not to think about it anymore.

"It can take you down a bad road," my father said out of nowhere. I assumed he was still talking about music.

"I did some things that ruined my life," he said while staring blankly at the field of dead grass, "and now look at me. Living in this piece of shit."

Instead of turning to look at the house in which he lived, I looked upwards into the bleached white sky above. I saw what I could become not from the life that my father lived, but from the life that he didn't. This moment burned an emptiness into my thoughts that would forever become a part of me. From that vacuum in my mind I constantly run, doing anything to avoid falling into that meaningless place within my life.

As we again drove down the gravel driveway, leaving my schizophrenic, alcoholic father, I forced my mind to think about the man from which it came.

THAT YEAR

Ten.
People yelling all around me.
Nine.
I'm yelling too.
Eight.
I'm stoned and thinking too much.
Seven.
What's the point?
Six.
Stop it.
Five.
Feeling good.
Four.
The same damn thing.
Three.
I'm yelling.
Two.
People yelling all around me.
One.
I'm alone.

THIS YEAR

Ashley and I are sitting on the roof of the shopping center in the middle of town. We can see the parking lot stretch off into the distance, with its empty spaces and its burning bright lights.

It's the new year.

We left someone's house and came here. We climbed some pipes in the back behind the dumpsters.

Black rooftop stretches out around us, spotted with different vents and fans and boxes. Some shoot out hot steam with a humming noise. Others sit silent.

We stare quietly at the town sitting below us, draped in the new year.

Nothing will change.

Everything will change.

I hold Ashley and I feel something like an empty happiness. I feel its outer shell surround me, but inside there is nothing. It's an empty feeling, but it's a feeling nonetheless.

She kisses me and I kiss her.

She touches me and I touch her.

We lie down on some old blankets we brought and stare at the sky above us. I keep feeling this empty happiness surrounding me. It touches my mind, but I don't let it become me. I can't let it become me. I just sit beside it and watch.

"What do you want?" Ashley asks me.

I lie without saying anything for a few minutes.

"I don't know," I tell her, "Something."

She lies without saying anything for a few minutes.

"Do you want me?" she asks.

"Yes," I say without waiting. Any silence would be an answer stronger than what I would say.

"You don't seem to. You don't seem to want anything."

I start to reply with something along the lines of how I love her, but I end up saying nothing at all.

She wraps her arms around me.

"I'm lost I guess," I tell her, "I want you. I do. But I need something. I feel like I'm dying."

She starts to speak, but stops before the words leave her mouth.

The sky above us feels old. I've known it for too long. I've always known it. I look closely at the stars and the blackness that surrounds them.

My life feels like a hole I've become trapped in for all time. Forever I've repeated everything I will ever do.

I'm born. I live. I die.

I'm born. I live. I die.

Forever.

I need to break myself forward into something unknown. Why? I don't know, but I can't let this pointlessness stop me anymore.

A loud slam comes from across the roof and flashlights shine in our direction.

Ashley gives me a look of fear. I'm not sure what look it is that I gave her, but I know that it was not fear. I pull her up and we're running.

We run fast across the black rooftops, in between the fans and the vents and the boxes. We're far down the roof now, in what seemed liked an instant. I can see flashlights shining in our direction, hitting the world around us. I pull her faster. My shadow shines, for a second, like a giant on the wall next to us.

Someone is yelling behind us. I don't listen. I just hear it as we keep running.

I laugh at the situation because I feel like a teenager running from some insignificant punishment that seems like the end of the world. To be caught would mean nothing, but to not get caught would mean everything.

We reach the end of the roof and with a few small jumps we're on the ground.

Trees surround us.

I feel the present moment move through my déjà vu and into my mind. The trees become apart of me. I'm surrounded by my life in all directions. We walk and I feel myself moving though this moment. I feel myself moving through moments I've moved through before. I watch my breath as it leaves in a cloud through the cold air and passes in front of the bright moon that hangs in the sky.

We're gone, somewhere else.

Ashley is breathing hard.

I'm laughing and feeling young.

"Fuck," I say smiling.

She doesn't say anything.

She looks at the ground as we walk home.

I need more of something.

Something in this.

I need myself.

SNOW

My stomach burns as I walk in the cold air of January. Every day I feel myself dying within the pain that controls my life. My thoughts are constantly centered upon it as I sense my fragile life falling apart day by day. I should learn from the pain and let it show me what I am. Instead I just grumble in loathing at it. I dream of not being in this body or in this life. I let the aching push me into misery.

This déjà vu that has engulfed my mind fuels my daily sorrow. Not because it causes it, but because it amplifies anything that I experience. When you sense that something lasts forever, you feel it more than normal. It pulses through every part of your consciousness and screams throughout your mind.

Forever.

My thoughts ramble on in disorder.

I never seem to make any sense, yet I understand everything that I think.

Snow is falling around me, creating a world of cold silence and solitude. I'm walking for no reason other than to get out of my apartment. I couldn't be inside anymore.

The sky is gray and the ground is white.

Dark brown trees sit with their bare branches covered in dull white snow.

I hear no one and see no one.

Burning. Stabbing. Cutting.

My stomach yells at me.

I can't take it.

I can't take this damn body.

I find a small bench to sit on that's somehow not covered in snow. The world is gray and white and full of nothing, which makes any sign of life stand out loudly against the barrenness of winter.

Silence.

I am all that exists.

This pain is all that exists.

I sit alone until my body is numb from the cold, until the pain in my stomach fades.

I pull out a cigarette and smoke it.

Why do I do this to myself?

I have no answer.

I question why anything happens at all. I question whether or not I bring bout everything on myself. Did I bring this pain into my life? Do I want this pain without me knowing it? Did I do something to deserve it?

I laugh at myself for being vain.

I laugh at myself for thinking that I'm God.

God doesn't exist and neither do I.

Or do I?

I walk home feeling empty.

I'm standing in my kitchen holding a bottle of beer in my hand. I take one drink and give up. I feel myself falling into somewhere I don't want to be. I go to bed and fade into a place where I won't exist.

MONTHS

Winter passes by as an empty crawl through time.
I may as well have been dead, but my life goes on.
My stomach hurts.
It gets better.
It hurts.
It gets better.
The déjà vu pulses throughout my life.
I've been here before.
I'll be here again.
Nothing happens.
Something happens.
Forever.
Days of work pile upon themselves in a blur.
It's getting warmer.
My mind is melting.
My thoughts are moving more freely.
My life is burning.
My stomach is burning.
I can't take this.
Something needs to happen.
Nothing happens.
Something needs to happen or I'll be here again.
A pain in my gut.
A pain in my head.
Déjà vu.

OUTSIDE

"I quit my job today," I tell Ashley.

"You quit your fucking job?" she replies loudly.

"Yea."

She stares at me behind eyes that say more than I can comprehend.

"What are you gonna do? You have a damn apartment. You have to stay alive you know? Eat food and stuff. Damnit. What the fuck are you gonna do?"

I stare out of the window. I'm going to do nothing.

"I'll be okay," I tell her.

"Yea," she says, "Sure."

The sun is shining.

I want to be outside.

My stomach hurts and I don't care.

"My lease is up in a month," I tell her, "I'm not signing it again."

"What?" she asks.

"My lease is up in a month," I tell her again, "I'm not signing it."

"Yea. I heard you," she says angrily, "So you're gonna be homeless now too?"

I can hear the sound of everything outside my apartment window.

I feel something.

Happy?

"I guess so," I tell her as I stare out the window at some people walking by down below.

We sit without talking.

I was going to work and I couldn't take it anymore.

Burning. Stabbing. Cutting.

Again.

I couldn't take it anymore.

I felt myself falling into a hole I'd fallen into forever.

I remembered all the times I told myself that I would change something and all the times I never did.

I couldn't take forever anymore.

"So what are you going to do?" she asks me.
"I'm going somewhere," I tell her.
"You're kidding."
"No."
"So you're just leaving?"
"Yea."
She gets up and heads toward the door.
"I'm leaving," she says.
"Don't," I tell her, "Please. Please don't be mad. I need this."

I'm talking without thinking about what's being said. It's not that I don't mean what I'm saying. I'm being sincere. I'm just not there for it. My mind is off somewhere else. I don't know where. It's just not here. I tell her something and she heads back.

She's sitting in front of me again.
"Are you coming back?" she asks me.

I stare out of the window at the sunlight shining on the wet grass. It's April. I look her in the eyes. I know this isn't being kind to her. I know that I'm being selfish, but I need this.

"Maybe. Probably," I say, "I don't know."
She keeps looking at me.
I keep looking at her.
"So you're just going to leave everyone?" she asks shaking her head. Tears are building up along the bottom of her eyes. I watch as they collapse into a teardrop that rolls down her face and rest along the bottom of her chin.

"I'm not leaving anyone besides you," I say, "You're the only person I have."

We sit staring at each other in silence. I can tell she's trying to think of what to say.

I feel bad.

She starts to really cry.

I rub the tears from her face and give a half smile. I can't think of anything to say. I want to tell her I love her. I do love her.

"I can't stay here anymore," I say.

"Why?" she asks, "Why do you need this? What do you need? What do you want?"

I look out the window at nothing in particular and then back into her eyes, which are now red from crying.

"I want something else. I need something else," I say, "I don't know what. I just know that it's not this."

She shakes her head.

I stare down at my feet and feel today sink in.

I quit my job, but the déjà vu is still here.

Have I done this before?

It feels so new, yet it feels so old.

Have I done everything before?

Will I always feel this way?

Have I reached the end of all possibilities?

I don't have an answer.

"I want to be alone," Ashley says.

I get up to leave, but she stands up before me and walks out the door.

I sit alone, like I always have and always will.

PART TWO

COLORS

It shines above me in every color.
I try to touch it, but I don't exist.
I feel sad because it's so beautiful.
Because it's so real.
They want to take it.
But I don't have it.
They want to exist.
But no one does.

It moves in spirals, falling to a place that isn't here.
I feel sad for being who I am.
For being who I'm not.
For being anything at all.

It fades out into everything, becoming nothing.
Rain pours down from the black sky.
They want it.
They need it.
But it's gone.

I feel nothing as I wake up to my empty bedroom.

FUTURELESS

I spend most of the time doing what I want, which is nothing. I live in an endless stream that flows within my consciousness.

I'm awake.
I'm asleep.
I'm awake.

I gave most of my things away. What I wanted to keep I stored away my brother's house. I told my family I was going somewhere to do something. I told them I was going somewhere to be someone. What I'm really doing is going nowhere to do nothing and to be no one.

I'm lying in the middle of my mostly empty apartment, staring at the ceiling fan spinning above me. The sun is out and shining through the windows. I can hear the sound of life outside and the spinning of the fan above me.

I'm leaving tomorrow.
I've got no plan.
I've got money saved up though.
I should have enough to get by for a while.
Maybe a year.
Maybe a month.
After that I'll have to come up with something.

Burning. Stabbing. Cutting.
It happens every day.
I feel like I'm dying.
I know that I'm dying.
I can't die until I'm alive though.

It happens every day.
Burning. Stabbing. Cutting.

Ashley comes over.

She said she wasn't going to leave me. She said that I was going to have to leave her.

She lies down next to me and stares at the ceiling fan too.

"Maybe you're right," she says, "Maybe you are crazy."

I don't reply.

I just laugh.

"Don't you think this is a little clichéd?" she asks.

"Yea," I tell her.

"It's like some bad movie," she says turning over to look at me, "You'll drive into the sunset while you realize something about life that no one else will understand."

I turn over to look at her.

She looks empty.

"Sounds good to me," I say with a smile.

She doesn't say anything. We stare at each other. We touch each other. Nothing happens.

She starts to cry.

"Spend tonight with me," she says.

I nod and wipe the tears from her face.

I don't feel a thing.

We spend the day doing nothing in my mostly empty apartment. We talk about depressing things like the way everybody sucks and how the world is falling apart and how I'm leaving everyone who loves me behind.

The sun begins to set and the apartment becomes filled with a golden light. I decide now would be a good time to leave. I tell Ashley to head out to the car. We'll go somewhere else tonight.

I can't stay here anymore.

She heads out to the car as I stand in the front doorway, looking at what use to be the place that I lived. I should feel sad, or at least feel something at all, but I don't.

I close the door and leave.

SPIRAL

There are lights in the distance.

We drive to them.

We've been falling through town without an idea of what to do or how to spend our last night together.

Crowds of people and rides and tents sit below the bright lights that have pulled us in. We decide to go, since we have nothing else to do.

The sun is sitting just out of sight, and the world around us is a dark blue that lives in between the washed out reds and yellows of the cheap fair lights. The sight and the sound and the smell of the world around me feels so familiar, yet unknown at the same time. It's as if I'm experiencing a newness that I've been acquainted with before. I remember the first time this sensation showed itself to me as I sat on the curb in front of my apartment. I feel exactly as I did then. I feel thrust into the middle of myself, into the middle of everything. The world feels both old and new.

Ashley grabs my hand and pulls me into the crowd of people. She buys us tickets to do whatever we want to do.

"I should have bought those," I tell her.

"You save your money for yourself," she says in a way that hides whether or not she's saying it out of love or disdain.

The first thing we do is ride a small carousel meant for children. She somehow talked the man operating it to let us on. I tell her that I don't want to, but she makes me. Parents stand alongside the ride watching us as we sit on the brightly painted horses that were meant for their children.

I look beside me at Ashley, who is riding a golden horse with eyes that have been faded away by years of use. She looks at me and laughs, which makes me laugh back. It's a genuine laugh. I feel it start deep within me and get pulled out by the sound of her happiness. I watch her smiling as her eyes reflect the colorful lights surrounding us.

I see her and her entire life all at once.

I see the way that she will never be with me again.

For a moment I feel sad.

The moment lasts forever.

We leave the carousel as the parents stare at us in contempt. I can't decide if it's because we corrupted the ride that was meant for their kids or because they wanted to ride it themselves.

I begin to feel young, as I did when we were running on the roof. I wonder whether or not that's all that I want. Am I just trying to ignore what my life will become? Am I just afraid of growing old? I don't have time to answer the questions. Ashley shoves me into another ride.

We spin in circles as the world around us blurs into rivers of light and movement. I laugh to myself over the fact that of all the times for my stomach to not be upset now is one of them.

I sit watching the world swirling around me for all eternity. Time moves forward but nothing else does. Movements mask life's true endlessness, as we sit forever spinning, going nowhere.

Ashley and I are sitting on the curb behind one of the rides. We're sharing a cigarette and talking of things that I forget about once they're said.

"I love you," she tells me after taking a long drag from the cigarette.

When I hear her say it I feel alone.

I'm not sure why.

She hands me the cigarette and I finish what's left.

"I love you too," I tell her.

We sit without talking until she breaks the silence.

"One more ride?" she asks.

I nod yes and we stand up.

We can't agree on what to ride and end up standing in the middle of a crowd of people, doing nothing.

"You should go," she tells me.

I look her in the eyes.

I almost tell her that I love her again but end up in silence. I wrap my arms around her and we stand holding each other in the middle of the crowd of people.

"You're alone now Ferris," she whispers into my ear as she lets go of me and walks away.

I'm left among the crowd of lights and sounds as emotions drift through me as they always have and always will.

I stand alone within forever.

STUCK

I'm moving towards something.

No.

Towards nothing.

I've been driving all night.

It's now early in the morning and the sun is just beginning to rise. It's a cloudy day, so the light becomes a dampened blue by the overcast sky.

I'm tired but nowhere near sleep. My mind is caught within thoughts of myself.

Where am I going?

What am I looking for?

I listen to the sound of the road below my car. It's an endless moan of movement that makes me feel depressed. The realization that I've left my old life behind begins to settle in. It brings nothing new, which makes me feel emptier than ever. I've left everything behind and still I feel stuck within my pointless life. The déjà vu rips painfully through my thoughts. I can feel it now, the sensation itself. Before it affected only what I experienced, but now I feel the impression it makes directly upon me. It burns within my mind and throws me into the present. It holds me in place and won't let me leave this life, this reality, behind.

Is it showing me something?

Is it making me see what's right here in front of me?

I remember I'm driving and move my attention back onto the road. I drive onto the next exit and stop at the closest gas station. I'm sitting in my car and feeling strange as questions fly throughout my thoughts. I let them go and just sit.

My mind begins to settle.

The sun has fully risen and the gray sky has engulfed the world. The sight of the rundown gas station sitting against the dreary sky makes me feel a hint of despair, and with it a small loneliness. For a moment I sit thinking about everyone I've known.

I decide I can't stay here anymore.

I decide that I can't be awake anymore.

I drive across the street to a small hotel that sits next to the interstate. The gray sky above keeps yelling though my mind, throwing depressing thoughts in every direction.

I walk into the main office. An older woman is sitting at the desk. She gives me a friendly look that makes me feel even worse.

I get a room and leave.

I'm standing in front of the door to my hotel room and I can't move. I just stand staring at the faded teal colored door. I can feel the emptiness behind it. I can feel the emptiness within myself. I'm stuck.

The sound of people talking in the distance shakes me awake and I break free from the nothing that was holding me in place. I use my key and open the door. Inside is a room decorated in cheap brown furniture and dirty tan wallpaper. I can smell the dusty carpet as I walk in. I shut the door and the room becomes dark, as if it was night.

I fall on the bed and sleep.

FROM NOTHING

I'm lying alone in the middle of somewhere.
I'm staring into her eyes.
Someone I used to love but never knew.
The way we exist begins to spin.
She tells me something.
I tell her everything.

I'm surrounded by people in the middle of nowhere.
I'm staring into her eyes.
Someone I never loved but always knew.
The way we exist begins to spin.
She tells me everything.
I tell her nothing.

I'm standing on the outside.
I'm staring into her eyes.
She's no one.
The way we exist begins to spin and never stops.
There's nothing to say.
There's nothing at all.

I wake up to the sound of my empty hotel room.

DUST

The streets around the hotel are empty, but the constant sound of the interstate makes it sound like a busy place. I woke up just as night fell and now I need something to do, so I walk across the road to a small liquor store that sits on the corner. I buy a case of cheap beer and a pack of cigarettes. The cashier tells me to have a good night and in my head I try think of a clever reply, but come up with nothing.

"You too," I say back to him.

I walk back to my room and pass no one on the way.

I'm sitting on the hotel bed, drinking beer and watching shitty television. With every drink I take I become more of a cynical asshole about everything.

I can't stand it.

I can't stand all the bullshit that people do.

I turn the television off and sit drinking in silence.

I can feel myself falling into the déjà vu. It sat quietly in my head for a while, but now I can feel it waking up and stretching itself out across my life.

This existence begins to intensify, as the sensation burns brighter in my mind. Again and again I sit here and drink while I fall deeper into myself. The room feels as if it was apart of me. It feels as if it's existed forever, just as I have.

I need to do something.

I need to escape.

I step outside to smoke but the feeling follows me. Now I'm standing on the balcony watching headlights fly past on the interstate as the entire world solidifies into eternity. Cars fly by as they always have, going places they've always been. I feel the future pulling the past towards itself as the present engulfs them both.

Why do I do this to myself? Do I really want to get somewhere? Or do I like tearing myself down in this pathetic life I live?

As I watch the traffic I think of where it is that I want to be. All that I can come up with is someplace with meaning. But all around me I see meaninglessness.

So I pitifully burn my life away.

I take a long drag from my cigarette and try to think of anything but what's happening. My mind wont let me. The déjà vu won't let me. No matter what I think, I'm thrust into the present.

These thoughts aren't my own. I just watch them as they live and die. It's the same with the world around me. Nothing exists for itself. It's all just a collision between something and nothing.

I catch my mind falling into confusion as I think more and more unintelligible thoughts. I go back inside and fall on the bed.

The more I drink the more this all confuses me, but at the same time I become more honest with myself with what's happening. I stand up to go take a piss and stumble a few times on the way to bathroom.

I stand laughing as I piss in the bathtub, an idea I got from being drunk. When I'm done I feel bad for a reason I can't decide upon, so I stand for a moment and think nothing.

I'm drinking again and smoking more cigarettes than I can keep count of. I try to stop my thoughts, but the room begins to spin when I do, so I continue thinking to myself to keep from falling into the spiraling world around me.

I get caught staring at the old carpet as it slowly moves around in my vision. I'm sinking deeper into something that I don't want to be.

I could die right now and be better off.

The thought of death scares me.

I keep drinking.

I don't want anything anymore.

I don't want to be here.
I don't want to go anywhere.
I don't want to exist.

But I don't want to die.

I fall down on the bed and stare at the ceiling as it stares back at me. My entire life shows itself to me through drunken memories.

It all looks pointless.

One thing happens and then another, without any reason behind any of it. Why do I need a fucking reason? A meaning can't really exist, so why do I want one so bad?

I'm laughing at myself and drinking and feeling awful about everything. My head is moving but I don't make it move. I'm standing in front of a mirror in the bathroom and I don't remember getting here. I'm staring at myself and talking out loud, but I don't know what I'm saying. My eyes are red and my hair is a mess and I look like I'm dying.

Burning. Stabbing. Cutting.

"Fuck," I say to no one.

"Fuck," I say to myself.

My stomach is killing me.

I fall down beside the bed and think about dying.

I can feel death and what it means to die.

I don't want this.

The room is spinning.

My thoughts are spinning.

I don't want die.

I don't want to live.

What do I want?

I climb into the bed and pass out.

GOING NOWHERE

I'm throwing up blood into a hotel toilet.
This is it.
My life is this.
Forever.

After I puke up everything within me I feel strangely okay. My stomach is fine while the rest of my body just feels weak. My mind, however, is missing. I try to think about anything at all, but I just end up fading out into the nothing that's taken over where my brain used to be.

I'm sitting on the end of the bed. The blinds are still pulled shut. From the sliver of light coming in through the sides of the window I can tell that the sky is cloudless.

I sit within the emptiness in my mind and stare blankly at the cheap brown carpet beneath my feet.

The déjà vu snaps me into place out of nowhere, and with it comes my lost mind. I realize that I'm sitting in a cheap hotel off of the interstate, and I have no plans of what to do next. I start to think about what it is that I want and what I can do to get there.

I neither want something nor nothing.
I want what's in between.
I want what doesn't exist.

I'm standing outside my room, staring at the cloudless blue sky and trying to figure out what to do. All I can come up with is to drive until I find some other hotel off the interstate.

The thought of it makes me feel depressed.

I left my entire life behind without an idea as to how to build a new one. I don't want a plan though. I'm done with any ideas of how life should be lived. They always fall through and leave you stuck with stupid habits and pointless ways of living your life. You end up heading towards a dream that had been dead before you even started.

So without a goal and a way to get to it, I give up and remain in the hotel. I call the office and tell them I'm staying another night.

I walk down the street and buy my breakfast from a gas station. I eat alone at a worn down picnic table that sits beside the hotel parking lot. The sun is shining and the trees sitting in the distance are beginning to turn green again. I can feel spring caressing life into the world which winter has possessed for some time now.

I look back at the hotel and the cars. I smell the smell of pavement and gasoline. I listen to the sound of traffic and of people talking.

I don't want this world made by other people to be the place that I live. Everything that I experience shapes who I become, and most of what I've experienced in life has come from other people. Am I mostly a product of other people's lives?

I need to escape it. It wasn't enough to leave my own life behind. I have to leave everyone's lives behind. The artificial world we've all created is pulling me down into state of being that tears at my soul.

I contemplate over that fact that for a moment I believed I had a soul. Do I believe that I do? Where is it then? What is it then?

I give up on the question and return back to thinking about what I must do. I'll drive west more, until I find somewhere I can stay that is separate from everywhere else, if any such place exists. I'll leave behind the man-made world and find a place where the self that I must find can exist without corruption.

I walk back to my hotel room in what seemed like an instant. I pull open the blinds so the entire room is lit up with the day's light. Sitting on the bed, I let my mind relax. I realize my déjà vu has been barely floating through my mind for a while now. Is it because I've truly decided something to do with my life? Is it because I'm taking my life in a direction it hasn't gone before?

As I ask myself these questions the déjà vu grows stronger again. I begin to feel confused, staring at the brightly lit hotel room and feeling like I've sat here forever. Questions enter my mind, but never take shape. The feeling of an unknown answer is the only sign that the questions even existed. For a moment I can see a piece of existence that escapes the déjà vu, and it exists within my thoughts. Before I can grasp it, it slips away into the familiar reality around me.

I sit and think for hours.

The sun is beginning to set.
How long have I been sitting here?
I step outside and stare at the world.
It's a place I've already left behind, and a place I'm beginning to find for the first time.
I go back inside and fall asleep to thoughts of everything.

FEEL

I'm lost. The people around me are too. We're talking to each other but no one can understand what's being said. We just feel emotion coming out from others. I look at her and I feel what it's like to love someone. The sound of something heavy echoes out from behind the trees. She pretends not to notice. Someone grabs me by the arm and now I'm sitting inside a flower that wraps its pink, shining petals around my body. I tell myself that this doesn't make sense, but then I tell myself that it does. The sound of something heavy echoes out from inside myself. She pretends not to notice. I look at her and I feel what it's like be alone. The walls around me open up to a place I've been before. People are running, covered in mud and screaming at everything around them. Someone grabs me by the arm and I feel what it's like to die. I look her in the eyes and I don't feel anything. The sound of something heavy is the only thing that is. Everyone is gone. The sound of something heavy is the only thing that is. I tell myself that this makes sense. The sound of something heavy is the only thing that is. I tell myself that it doesn't. The sound is gone. She pretends not to notice. The people around me do too. No one is talking to anybody. We don't feel anything. I'm lost. She pretends not to exist as I wake up to the familiar life I live.

THE PUSH AND THE PULL

I'm driving towards the future, which is really just the present cloaked the veils of movement and mind. It's early in the morning, on what I think may be a Sunday. The sky is again clear, and the sun is just beginning to rise. In front of me the world is a dark blue that fades into a lightness the further back it moves behind me. I look in my mirror and see a golden line of light along the horizon. The sight of it feels familiar, as does everything else that I experience.

I watch as my mind fades into nothing and the road in front of me becomes the entirety of my being.

I do this for days.

I drive.

I sleep.

I drive.

Sometimes I sleep at cheap hotels.

Sometimes I sleep in my car.

The world becomes less flat the farther I go.

Sometimes I stop and watch the clouds move by in the sky. I can feel my life moving forward but never really moving at all. Everything is static.

Some days it rains and some days it doesn't.

I wonder where it is I'm going.

Am I going anywhere?

I drive.

I sleep.

I drive.

Sometimes there's a burning in my stomach.

I watch the pain as it takes over my thoughts.

Sometimes I don't drive.

I just sit inside wherever it is I'm at and turn myself off. I think about drinking, but I don't. I can't. I won't.

I drive.

I sleep.

I drive.

Sometimes I don't sleep.

I move through life with sleepless eyes and sleepless thoughts.

I drive.

I drive.

I drive.

Sometimes I talk to myself.

Sometimes I talk to the world. I tell it that I don't understand. I ask it what it's like to die. It tells me nothing and I think that's the answer.

Sometimes I turn around and drive back the way I came, just to see what it feels like. I think of my old life and what it would be like to be there again. I ask myself whether or not I'll ever return.

I don't have an answer.

Sometimes I turn on the radio and listen to static. It sounds more beautiful than the music that it could play. Endless noise that sounds real.

Sometimes I talk to people.

Usually I don't.

I drive.

I sleep.

I drive.

I am the concrete.

I am the paint.

I am the movement.

I am everything but alive.

I drive.

I sleep.

I drive.

I look for signs of places that I want to go, but never find them, so I keep on driving.

I wonder how far I'll go.

I wonder how long I'll live.

I wonder how I'll die.

Sometimes I don't think I'll ever die.

Burning. Stabbing. Cutting.

Sometimes I think that I am dying.

I drive.

I sleep.

I drive.

The sensation in my mind of being where I've always been, of doing what I've always done, constantly pushes me into reality. I can't escape this life no matter how hard I try.

Sometimes I think of killing myself.

Sometimes my car turns into a concrete wall.

I smash myself into nothing.

But I know that I wont and I know that I don't want to and I know that I never really even thought of doing it in the first place.

I drive.
I sleep.
I drive.

I drive.
I sleep.
I drive.

I drive.
I sleep.
I drive.

The words stop making sense.
Though they never really did.

ELSE

I bought five joints from a guy at a gas station. He asked me if I wanted some grass. I didn't think people still called it grass.

Now I'm stoned and lost in the woods a mile or two behind the strip mall I left my car at.

I stole a cheap backpack from a department store. I just put it on and walked out.

I'm sitting on a rock and looking in my bag at the cans of fruit and the little bars made of things I most likely can't digest.

I stole those too.

There's also a first-aid kit, a canteen, a notebook and pens, a compass, a knife, and a small bottle of whiskey, just in case.

I didn't steal those. I was beginning to feel like I was pushing my luck, and theft wasn't really my thing anyway. It wasn't that I felt bad. I could care less about the damn department stores. They have plenty of other things to sell. I know this because I spent the last three years of my life stacking stuff on shelves.

Inside the first-aid kit are the four joints I have left.

I laughed to myself when I put them there.
I was stoned.

I still am.

Even though I'm lost, I feel as though I've been here before. I'm in the middle of nowhere, someplace I've never been, and I feel as if I've never been anywhere else.

I decide that I must be wrong.

I must be in the middle of somewhere.

Somewhere I've always been.

I also decide that I must be the very last living thing to ever exist. The universe has reached the end of all possibilities and I am the last thing that it had to do.

There's nothing left that's new.

I feel down over the fact that there is nothing left to do that hasn't been done. I also feel down because I got last pick for the universe's choice of existence.

Or maybe I'm the first thing to exist. Maybe everything has been done, and so existence is repeating itself to the beginning, which is my life. If what I'm doing has been done before, then obviously I couldn't be the last thing to exist.

"I must be the first!" I yell to myself.

This made me feel somewhat better, but only somewhat. There's still nothing left to do that hasn't been done. And now I have the rest of everything else to look forward to, again.

"But time doesn't exist," I tell myself, "and neither do I."

The sunlight cuts through the trees above and shines warm on my back

"If time doesn't exist," I say out loud before I move my thoughts back inside my head.

If time doesn't exist, then there is no beginning or end. I know that time doesn't exist. I've seen it for what it is.

Movement.

Collisions.

Thoughts.

Life and death.

I sit confused for a moment. I'm not sure anything I just thought makes any sense, so I start over.

"If time doesn't exist," I say out loud to the rock below me, "then there is no beginning or end. And I know that time does not exist. It's an illusion caused by the ever-moving present. If there is no beginning or end, then there is infinity. If there is infinity, then there is no limit to the possibilities. If there's no limit to the possibilities of existence, then there's still hope for me to change my life and escape the hole that I'm in. Just because existence is limitless, doesn't mean that it doesn't repeat itself. But since there is no time, nothing's been done before, and nothing can repeat. It's always been done actually, and always will be. That means that the infinite amount of things that can happen have already happened, are happening, and will happen. So what is this déjà vu? A break in time? A glimpse into reality? No. It's all just meaningless words. I lost it all at infinity."

I jump down from the rock and stare at it.

It says nothing back, which is probably a good thing.

I try to write down what I just said, but forget most of it by the time I get my notebook out. I end up drawing pictures of the trees around me and giving up halfway through because they don't really resemble trees at all.

My mouth begins to feel painfully dry, so I take out the canteen and drink some water. After a little while I realize that I drank all of it, and now all that I have left to drink is the bottle of whiskey.

I laugh.

What the hell was I planning?

I was driving and couldn't take it anymore. I had to get somewhere. I ended up at a rest stop, looking through a wall of brochures for someplace to go, somewhere to be alone. Most of them advertised places you could pretend to be alone, but not really be alone because other people were hiding all around you pretending to be alone too.

I gave up on the brochures and everything else. I decided I would just leave my car somewhere, stock up on supplies, and walk into the woods. I had nothing left to lose. I had to be alone. I had to find seclusion. I had to leave the road behind. I was done with it.

I left my car parked in a strip mall. Behind it I could see what at least looked like a wooded area stretching on for quite awhile, so I figured I should just head out. My car would most likely get towed, but didn't care. Maybe I should just start walking everywhere anyway.

So I walked behind the strip mall and lit up one of the joints I got from the guy at the gas station.

"It's some good shit," he told me.

I was walking through the woods, getting stoned, and listening to the artificial world behind me fading away. I didn't know what was ahead of me. It could be wilderness or it could lead straight back into society. I didn't care, as long as it was somewhere else.

What it led me to was this rock.

I do feel secluded. I do feel alone. But I still feel trapped in the life I was living before.

So now I have to decide what to do.

I brought one bottle of water and already drank it all. Maybe I should just stay here and dehydrate myself. Or I could drink the bottle of whiskey and fall off a cliff somewhere. Why didn't I bring more water? I've got no plans of what to do, so I sit here and think about whatever thoughts come to my mind.

I realize I'm lost and alone in unfamiliar woods, without any water, and the sun is beginning to disappear.

I laugh at myself and everything else.

The feeling of someone behind me creeps through my body.

I turn and no one is there.

My hands begin to feel as if they don't exist, and then my arms begin to fade away as well.

I'm becoming paranoid about something I don't understand. My arms are still non-existent even though I can see they're still attached to my shoulders. I scratch my skin just to feel a sensation in my limbs. I look at my fingernails, which have grown long since I left behind my life in society. Small clumps of black dirt lie beneath them.

Are these really my hands?

Or do they belong to whomever it is that's sitting behind me? That non-existent being that watches everything that I do, just as it watches me now. I turn around again and see the trees shining gold from the setting sun.

I turn my vision back towards the hands that are no longer my own. I hold them up, silhouetting them against the sky. I've seen them here before, hanging in dark contrast to the golden scene behind them.

I know that I have.

It's not just a feeling.

It's a pure memory of this happening before, of being in this exact place and time.

The paranoia fades as I find comfort in this moment of forever. I realize I'm becoming attached to the déjà vu, to the feeling of never being somewhere new.

Am I looking in the wrong direction?

Instead of looking for something new, should I instead be looking deeper into what's already here?

I lose myself in the present until the sun is no longer. The sound of nowhere flows into my mind. Blue light, shining from the full moon above, swims between the trees and into my eyes. It brings with it a feeling of being within a dream.

No.

It doesn't create the feeling, but releases it from reality's grip. Nothing here is permanent. Nothing here is what it seems to be, and of this I am a part. The dream cannot exist without the dreamer, and the dreamer cannot exist without the dream. Without other, we are nothing. It's the collision, the point in which we experience, that is real.

No.

Not real.

It just is.

Reality is too much of a word to have any real meaning.

The wind blows through the leaves above my head. I feel the sound move into my senses and create the world around me. My thoughts ramble on, just as I do through the woods.

Burning.

A pain begins in my stomach.

Stabbing.

It's a familiar pain.

Cutting.

"Fuck off," I tell my body.

It tells me to fuck off too, only it says it in the way my stomach attacks my senses.

My head begins to feel weak.

My hands go numb.

I remember throwing up blood while snow fell around me. I remember thinking I was dying.

Now I'm standing in the middle of nowhere, thinking the same thoughts I did then. This time though, I'm certain that my body is ending this life that I'm living.

My legs feel weak, so I sit down on the ground where I was standing. I feel my pants get damp in the mud. I feel myself being pulled in two directions. I move deeper into feeling the pain within my body, yet at the same time I fade out of existence.

What a cruel fucking joke it is to be alive, to be aware of the death of everything and everyone you'll ever know, including yourself.

I begin to cry. At first I feel myself getting choked up over the thought of death. I think of the people I've known, of the life I've lived, and of the way none of it matters. The reality of impermanence floats into my thoughts and pushes me deeper into my sadness. Tears burst forth that I cannot control. I feel pathetic, sitting alone, crying over the death of everything.

My despair reaches its end and snaps, shooting me against the walls in my head. Shattering through the barriers of my emotion, I am thrust into the opposite side of my mind. I laugh at the tears upon my face and the endless transience of being.

I stand up and stare into the distance.
I see nothing.

BENEATH

I wasn't asleep.

I haven't slept for some time.

I was awake, but somewhere else.

My mind was caught in the space between here and there.

Here being me and there being everything else.

Now I'm staring at the graffiti that's painted in red on the concrete wall of the overpass that I'm sitting under. In large, barely legible letters it tells me

GO FUCK YOURSELF.

I think about it for a moment, and realize that in a way I am fucking myself.

I'm doing all this just to make myself feel better about the shitty way my life has played out. Over and over again I touch the deepest parts of my being just to see what I'm made out of, what I feel like.

All that I've come up with is emptiness.

I try to fill that emptiness with something sacred, but nothing sacred exists. Instead I force in lies made from thoughts that know only themselves.

The déjà vu pushes me into place.

I feel pathetic over the way that I've become so narcissistic. All the pain that I bring myself comes from my own selfishness. I reach for a meaning in my life, while ignoring everyone else's.

Am I going in the wrong direction?

Is the abandonment of self the only way to actually find meaning in life?

I feel weak at the thought of helping others. This gnawing at the deepest parts of my being blocks my way to compassion. How can I feel love for a world that I do not understand, that I do not even know is real?

I try to go back to the place in which I didn't exist, where awareness was all that was, but my discouraging thoughts have too strong of a hold upon me.

I sit thinking about myself because I don't know what else to think about. I've left behind society and my old life, yet still I'm stuck within this cycle of existence that's been pulling me along for all eternity. Maybe I'm just seeing the inevitable experience of forever?

It's all been done and there is no escape.

All that you can do is accept it.

The sound of moving cars from above pulls me back into the world in which I live in. I've wandered for days through places that meant nothing. For a while I was surrounded only by woods, without water and without direction. I enjoyed the silence and the escape from other people. My mind never rested though. Ceaselessly my thoughts brought up questions that meant nothing.

Last night, as I was walking through the dark woods lit only by the moonlight, I ran up against a highway. I walked along the road until I saw a gas station. It was closed, but in front was a brightly lit vending machine. From my wallet I took two crumpled dollar bills, and spent the next five minutes trying to get the machine to accept them. Eventually I was able to get two bottles of water, which I drank before even leaving the vending machine's side.

I wandered down the road in the direction I thought would lead me back to where I started.

I've been walking along for two days since then.

I haven't slept in four.

The setting sun is beginning to disappear behind the horizon, and the golden light that shined upon everything has begun to turn into a deep, blue glow. In the distance, behind the silhouetted shapes of the trees that lie in front of me, a glowing pink light drifts in place of the departed sun.

My eyes begin to shut.

My thoughts struggle to exist.

I feel as if I've always been lying beneath this overpass, falling asleep to the dying sunlight.

Will I wake up?

TOGETHER

The bees.
Made of concrete.
Fly above me, never stopping.

I'm making this happen.
All of it.
It's just a story I tell myself.

Never stopping, never starting.

The water.
Cold from their eyes.
Moves below me, always changing.

I'm making this happen.
Or am I?

Never stopping, never starting.

The fires.
Hot from silence.
Burn through me, always, and never.

All of it.

Never stopping, never starting.
Never, and always.

I awake to the sunlight in my eyes.

DROPS

Every part of me is soaking wet.

The only thing I have that's dry is the first-aid kit with four joints inside. It's sitting, wrapped in a plastic bag, inside my backpack.

It started raining yesterday morning while I was walking alongside the road that would lead me somewhere, and it hasn't stopped since. My clothes are damp and clinging to my skin. My feet sit in pools of water inside my shoes.

I look above to the gray sky. It drops endless water down into the damp green world that I am in. Cars fly past without seeming to notice me. Do I even exist? I can't remember the last time I talked to anyone. I think about how easy it was for me to steal the backpack and supplies. Have I finally become a ghost? Have I shoved myself out of the existence I was in?

The man selling pot at the gas station.

That was the last person I talked to.

"It's some good shit," he told me.

I walk through the rain in the direction I think will lead me to where I left my car. Street signs tell me I'm getting closer. As I walk down a road that leads me into town, a car cuts close by and honks at me through the rain.

I suppose that I am still here.

Or there.

I can't decide.

I watch my feet move across the wet pavement of the sidewalks. Forever these legs will walk through this dreary, concrete landscape. The déjà vu stabs my senses and I have to sit down in the grass along the sidewalk. My stomach begins to ache and my head begins to feel light.

I'm dying.

Again.

Forever.

No.

I stand up feeling fine within a few moments and head on my way.

What is wrong with me?

Nothing within my mind or body makes any sense.

In the distance I can make out the strip mall in which I left my car five days ago. I'm prepared for it to no longer be there. In fact, I don't want it to be there. I don't want anything to be there. I hope that when I walk around the corner I find a hole within reality, a place where nothing exists.

I walk into the parking lot and see it. My car is sitting right where I left it, without even a notice stuck upon it. I begin to feel something growing inside of my thoughts as I walk closer to the red automobile from nineteen-ninety-something.

It's an anger at what exists.

I can't stop it.

I stand in front of my car.

The red car from nineteen-ninety-something.

I stare at it.

It stares at me.

I break.

I yell.

I don't pay attention to whether or not people notice me, but I'm sure that they do. I'm screaming out loud at my life left sitting in the form of the red car that's been deserted in the same place, forever. I scream out things that don't make any sense. I scream out words that don't even exist.

I don't stop yelling as I find my keys, unlock the door, and get in the car. I continue to scream as I smash the horn on the steering wheel in front of me. Endless pure noise envelops everything.

I finally stop as I turn on the car.

It starts as if I had never left it.

I laugh.

I fucking laugh.

Why the hell not?

In the face of this existence, at least there's always the comedy of it all, the eternal joke of tragedy. I pull out a joint from my first-aid kit and light it on my car's built in lighter.

"Thanks," I tell the red car from nineteen-ninety-something. It was the first time I had used the little lighter that sat in the console of my car.

I sit with my car running, listening to the rain fall upon the roof in endless little thuds. I decide to leave the car behind. I'll take a train or a bus or anything that can move. I'll go west until I hit the coast. I can't drive anymore. I can't see this car anymore.

I get out and stand, again, in the rain.

My déjà vu stops me still as I look upward at the dark gray sky and watch the raindrops as they fly downward towards the ground in fast white dashes. They fall in my eyes and onto my skin.

I'm stuck gazing at this endless movement.

It exists in only one point in time.

Yet it moves as if there was no now, as if the past and the future were all that exists.

Pointless questions attack my thoughts.

I force myself to shove them out of my head, just to make a move. These endless questions in my mind get me nowhere. The more I think about this life, the less I know about it.

I pull my vision downwards and into the car. I grab my suitcase and a picture of Ashley that sat hidden underneath it. It was a picture of her that she took herself. Half of her face was cut out of the frame, and what was left in was out of focus. Still, the sight of it rings throughout me and becomes amplified through the increasing déjà vu in my mind. I stare at it as I stand up and leave the car.

Droplets of rain slowly gather upon the picture. I stare at my past and at the future that will never be. I begin to feel miserable, although I don't know why. I don't want the life that I lived, and I don't want the life that I've lost.

Yet with every raindrop that falls around me, deeper I move into sadness. What am I doing here in this loneliness?

I remember the hotel I passed as I walked back into town. I head in the direction of a place I can be alone. A place I can clean myself and sleep. A place I can be born into another day's life.

A place that isn't this.

PART THREE

WITH

She whispers, into my ear, words that don't exist.
I can feel them.
The way they move.
They watch us as we die.
"Did we make it?" someone asks.
"Make what?"
That.
The world around me creates itself.
"Oh."
Nothing.
They stare at me.
"Did you do it?"
I'm asleep.
I see it.
"Oh"
Flying.
Dreaming.
She whispers into my ear.
Words that exist.
"Don't close your eyes."
Did I make this all happen?
Look.
It's real.
I close my eyes.
I'm awake?
She whispers, into my ear, words that don't exist.
"Did I make it?" I ask.
"Make what?" she asks back.
That.
I'm awake.

NOTHING

My mind is in the same place it was when I began this.

Nowhere.

I stand in the shower until the hot water turns my skin red. I feel tired of this life, but my déjà vu won't let me quit. Constantly it throws me back into being.

I gather up the things I need.

Some clothes, my first aid kit, my backpack, and the picture of Ashley.

I leave the hotel room and walk outside to a sky that can't decide between the clouds or the sun.

I take an hour-long bus ride to the nearest train station. I sit beside the windows, watching the moving horizon in the distance. Nothing happens at all.

I arrive at the station, buy my ticket, and wait. It comes in a low rumble, followed by the loud scream of its whistle. I board the train and sit dazed in my seat. My body and mind have become broken down. My life has become an exhausting blur. The train begins to lurch forward, and within its movement I feel the endless toil of the future grabbing our lives and never giving us a moment of peace. Forever it pulls us away, yet it takes us nowhere.

WAVES

I'd been on the train for almost two days. Most of the time I slept. I never talked to anyone. I just sat alone, staring out of the window, swimming between the waking world and dreaming.

Now I'm standing in the train station without an idea of what to do. I walk out into the sunshine that falls from the clear blue sky. Without a plan I move down the street in a melancholy pace.

I've reached the end, and I've got nothing to do.

As I walk through these streets I feel the familiarity of this place grow within me. I know for a fact that during this life I have never been here before, yet I feel as if I've never been anywhere else. The bright reflections of the sky upon the shop windows, the strong shadows sitting out of reach from sun's light, the people that move in blurs around me. It all feels old.

I walk with my eyes fixed upon ground.

What was I looking for? A different place doesn't mean a different life. I'm still the same person, on the same planet, in the same existence.

My soul, which may or may not exist, sinks deep down into the endless hole within myself. I feel life's weight pushing upon my shoulders. Contradicting my surroundings, I sit deep within the darkest spots of my mind as I move throughout the sunny landscape.

I follow signs that point to the coast.

I dream in my head of seeing the ocean.

I'll walk into its waters.
I'll drift out into the universe.
I'll lose myself.
I'll become free.
I'll die.

The buildings begin to become sparse as I leave the city and walk along a road that supposedly leads me to the sea. The wind blows strong, creating a rustle in the tall plants to my side. Their leaves brush against me, caressing out a small comfort within my thoughts. Nature's eternal indifference is more genuine than any emotion man could create.

I walk along without a thought.
I can feel it getting closer.
I can smell it.
I can hear it.
I can see it.
It goes on forever, like everything else.
It belongs in eternity, like everything else.

My feet sit in the water as I stand staring out at the endless blue in front of me. I close my eyes and watch the sunlight shine through my eyelids, creating another world within my vision. The sound of waves floats in and out of my ears, giving life to the place inside my head.

I live there.
I die there.

I open my eyes and see what appears to be reality. Everything I experience, I have experienced before. The vast ocean that lies in front of me looks old and known, yet its existence is boundless.

My life is an echo of the sea.
Its endlessness exists in one moment, as does mine.
Every limitless part of it is connected into one.
Always here and now.
I think of the life I've lived up to this very point. I think of the people that have come and gone. I think of the things I've done, the things I've felt, and the things I've believed. In the face of this endlessness that lies in front of me, every part of my past dissolves into nothing.

Into everything.
Into what is and always will be.

A small cloud floats in front of the sun, creating a shadow upon the place that I stand.

This is it.
There is nothing else.
There is no answer.
There is no reason.
There is no meaning.
Just this.

The sound of water.

DRIFT

I'm drunk and stoned and killing myself.
I'm talking to people.
People I don't know.
She asked me a question.
I told her an answer.
Am I awake?
Yes.
Someone shoves me.
I shove them back.
I'm outside.
Déjà vu?
Streetlights.
Cars.
The sidewalk shakes in my vision.
I feel the concrete with my hand.
To my left is the sound of forever.
I'm somewhere.
Alone.
Crying.
An alley.
What am I doing here?
There isn't an answer.
The spinning goes on forever.
Burning. Stabbing. Cutting.
Forever.
I'm moving again.
People walk past, or I walk past them.
Alone, again.
I can feel the water at my ankles.
I'm smoking.
I'm killing myself.
I found the answer.
And it didn't exist.
So what now?
Accept this?
I laugh.

Or give up?
Become someone else in the endless sea.
Streetlights.
Darkness.
The sound of cars.
Meaningless.
So why care?
Float away into nothing.
Cold concrete beneath my hands.
Become anything but something.
The sound of cars.
Nothing.

I open my eyes in confusion.

The sun hasn't risen yet, but a faint violet light moves through the sky, hinting at its arrival. I stand up and feel the blood flow down from my head. I fall to the side and catch myself upon a railing. I close my eyes and brace myself.

Burning.
Stabbing.
Cutting.

I stand in place until my body is able to move without collapsing onto the concrete. Again, it's today. Again, I feel the ceaselessness of my life. The futility screams at me from every corner of my vision.

I'm alone behind an abandoned building. I must have ended up here last night.

I don't remember much.

I broke down and gave up.

I told myself that didn't care about dying, about anything.

But I did.

I want this life to become something more than a pointless moment in forever, but the meaning that I desire doesn't exist. No matter how hard I tried to look within this life, to look through it, I saw nothing.

And so I broke down even more.

My body feels like hell.
I walk out into the street.
Burning.
Stabbing.
Cutting.
I brace myself again until the nausea passes. In the distance I can hear the sound of early morning traffic.

Life plays its endless noise into my ears as I walk along the sidewalk without a direction in mind. The sky dances from violet to blue as more of the sun's light shines in from the east.

I feel sand below my feet.
The ocean stares at me as I stare at it.
Inside I feel a strange pain growing. It starts in my stomach and shoots upwards to my head.
Burning.
I fall down.
Stabbing.
The pain grows.
Cutting.
My insides spill out of my mouth.
The white sand becomes red with blood.
A shock moves through my body and I'm thrust into a place unknown to me.
It's gone.
My blood upon the sand confuses me.
Its color is unfamiliar.
The sensation is gone.
The déjà vu has disappeared.
I turn my head upward to the sea.
Sunlight is flooding into the world.
The sound of the waves makes me weak.
I'm lost.
I'm helpless.
Screaming at me from every direction is this existence of which I am a part. I can feel my life creating

itself before me, in ways that haven't been done before. My thoughts spill out words that I don't understand.

Burning. Stabbing. Cutting.

Again I throw up.

My hands are numb.

I feel fear.

It's a fear of the unknown, a fear of the death that I can now see existing within everything.

The déjà vu has ripped itself away, and left me stranded within this unfamiliar place. I'm afloat in the endless sea of being, and its ceaseless unknown waters frighten me. I'm just a droplet in an ever-changing sea of emptiness.

I stand up and feel my body begin to go numb.

My vision blurs.

I'm walking up the beach, towards the rising sun.

I can feel myself fading away.

Am I dying?

My fear grows stronger as I think of no longer existing.

"This is what you wanted isn't it?" I ask myself out loud.

Gravity becomes too much.

I fall down to my knees.

Concrete scrapes the skin off of my hands. The pain reminds me that I'm alive. It reminds me that I will die.

I watch the fear crumble as I let everything go.

I am nothing.

I am free.

The sky captures all of my vision as I roll onto my back.

A deep bright blue.

The sound of nowhere.

My eyes begin to close.

Is this it?

I watch forever end.

PART FOUR

SEPTEMBER

Golden leaves dance in front of the pale blue sky.
A single white cloud floats alone above.
This is nowhere.
This is here.

I died next to the sea.
I was born the same day.
I saw the endless flow of life within me.
No beginning.
No end.

I no longer feel the déjà vu that became the entirety of my life nearly a year ago, yet the memory of what it showed me remains strong within my mind. I know of the endlessness, the emptiness, behind everything. It no longer tears at my thoughts to know these things, however. I have become, from the inspiration of nature, indifferent to the matter. I live not within the hopes of the answer, but in the beauty of the question.

To say that I am no longer without despair would be a lie. To exist at all is to suffer. And I feel the suffering much deeper, albeit less violently, than I did before. The pain seeps within my mind, yet I don't let it take ahold. I watch it as it dies, like everything else.

Children run past behind me, scraping sticks upon the sidewalk as they move. I listen to the scratching, and their voices, fade away into the distance.

I was nothing.
I was forever within a singe moment, just as I had always been.
My eyes opened to a white room.
I was alone.

Happiness shows itself to me more often than it did before. The way light plays on objects, sounds float into my ears, smells arise from the world. These all bring contentment to my life, not an inward escape as they did before. The déjà vu had thrust me deep within this experience of being, and its departure didn't release me back into the disconnected way I lived before the sensation overtook my life. It left me, instead, fully drowned in existence. I immerse myself in what is there in front of me and inside of me. I don't attach to the feeling, however. I let it flow in and out of my head, as I do the pain.

I feel a aching in my stomach.
I stare at my feet and feel human.
I'm alive.

People surrounded me in the white room. The room was in a hospital. They told me I was found lying unconscious next to the beach. There was blood on my clothes and the ground beneath me.
They brought me here.
They asked me about myself.
I told them I was traveling.
They said they found something.
They said they needed to do some tests.
I let them.

Ashley doesn't live here anymore. Her father died and she moved back to the place that she was from.
I called her when returned.
She told me she thought I was dead.
I told her I was.
I could hear the way she held back her tears as she said good-bye.

I'm walking down the sidewalks that I've walked all my life. I stare down at my feet, watching the cracks in the pavement move through my vision. Dead leaves scatter the concrete and blow along in the calm wind.

They said it's in my stomach.
And other places too.

I moved into my brother's house.
He made his attic into a bedroom, which he lets me stay in. A tall oak tree, which turns bright red in the fall, sits just outside the window. When it rains I sit for hours watching and listening to the water drip among its branches. When the sun sets on a clear day, the golden light shines through the red leaves, creating a bright, warm glow of colors within my room.
I spend my days creating.
I write about what I've done and what I think and what I feel and what I know. I paint things that don't exist and things that do. I make music that no one will listen to, and then listen to it for days.
Most of the time I do nothing at all besides exist.

I'm sitting on the curb, thinking about dying. I often catch myself wondering what will happen. I've seen what lies beneath this place. I know I'll be here again, or better yet, never really leave. But is there anywhere else? Will I live every life that there is to live? Or will I always be this?
I let the questions go.
The answers don't exist.
I fall back into the place that I'm in, and watch the light from the sunset fall across the street in front of me.

The doctor sat beside me as I stared at the white ceiling of the white hospital room. He told me that I could live for a few months or maybe even a year, since I was young. I said nothing back. I just thought to myself of how I would have to die again.

I look upwards to the dark blue sky.
The sun is almost gone.
My body feels weak.
The sound of life moves through the air.

What is this?
Something.
Nothing.

This.

Now and again, I live and I die.